Dr. Adams *and* Master Death

Dr. Adams *and* Master Death

A PHILOSOPHICAL NOVEL

Michael H. Mitias

RESOURCE *Publications* · Eugene, Oregon

DR. ADAMS AND MASTER DEATH
A Philosophical Novel

Resource Publications
An Imprint of Wipf and Stock Publishers
199 W. 8th Ave., Suite 3
Eugene, OR 97401

www.wipfandstock.com

PAPERBACK ISBN: 978-1-6667-3733-2
HARDCOVER ISBN: 978-1-6667-9664-3
EBOOK ISBN: 978-1-6667-9665-0

JANUARY 5, 2022 1:53 PM

In Honor of John Quincy Adams
Teacher
Millsaps College 1965–1995

Contents

ONE

Master Death Visits Dr. Adams | 1

TWO

Liberal Arts Education | 29

THREE

David Meets Eve | 59

FOUR

David and Eve Fall in Love | 91

FIVE

Master Death's Last Visit to Dr. Adams | 116

ONE

Master Death Visits Dr. Adams

"How does it feel to stand on the Edge . . . yes, the edge of all edges? Did you envision, or even expect, that one day you would stand on this edge? Have you ever conceived or imagined what it would be like to stand on the Edge?" the stranger said with an obvious air of sarcasm, "How do you feel when you know that your left foot is hanging on the abyss of nonbeing and that your right foot will soon weaken and slowly slide into that abyss? Have you ever thought about the impending possibility that every bone, every nerve, every muscle, and every beat of your heart will soon tremble and then splinter into nothing?" The stranger paused, grinned sardonically, and continued haughtily, "Have you considered the possibility that the ideas you used to communicate to your students, to your colleagues, and to the philosophical community about the absoluteness and eternity of Truth, Goodness, and Beauty will soon lose their brilliance and pass into the darkness of that abyss? Did it occur to you that when you stand, as you are now standing, on the Edge that you will not any longer be able to desire, hope, aspire, dream, or create? Yes, Dr. Adams, how does it feel to be caught in the churning wheel of permanent transition, to be pricked by its ruthless spikes, and to feel dizzy by its endless motion? How does it feel to know that you will not any longer be able to stand on the peak of that mount, the mount of human existence, where Plato, Petrarch, Hegel, and many silly dreamers like you stood, and to contemplate the sunrise every morning and the sunset every evening and delight in the grandeur, glory, and splendor of the One? Wasn't this contemplation the reason for your being the illustrious Dr. Adams? Wasn't it the source of the inspiration that illuminated every step of your life? And now, yes now, standing on the Edge—have you a desire to contemplate the One? You loved light, especially the light of reason. You were charmed by its ultimate source, not by the source of this or that light, not even by the light of reason, but by the light of the One, the source of all light and all being—and now how does it feel to live in the darkness of the world you loved so much?" More than once Dr. Adams tried to interrupt the stranger who had invaded the privacy of his room and begun to lecture him on his impending extinction, but the stranger smiled and, motioning with his right hand, asked him to be patient!

"Do you remember how, in one of your inspired lectures to your innocent students—and I attended most of your lectures—you argued that a life worth living is a life of creation and giving, of living from the truth and in the warmth of the human heart? Do you also remember how soon after you uttered this profound statement that you sank into a momentary trance and emerged from it with the following gem of insight: 'A vision of the Source that gave rise to this mysterious, magnificent, and lovable universe is the most precious achievement a human being can aspire to in her life, and a life that does not seek to have this kind of vision is not worth living because,' you asked, 'how can we lead a human way of life, one worthy of our humanity, if it is not founded in this kind of vision? The question is not simply to exist but to exist as a human being. Has it occurred to you that humanity is a divine ray of light? Light is its source, and light is its destiny. How can we realize our destiny in the dark?'

"Oh, that was a splendid lecture! I wondered then whether you or the spirit in you delivered that lecture. I shall not dwell on this question, not with an illustrious philosopher such as you. My aim today is to dwell on your present predicament!" Dr. Adams's eyes were glittering with curiosity, impatience, and awkwardness. His lips were quivering with obvious tension. His only solace was that this stranger was speaking with some knowledge of philosophy, but it was clear to the stranger that Dr. Adams was desirous to speak, but the stranger obstructed his desire again.

"A lover of light is a lover of life. You are a lover of light; therefore, you are a lover of life. This kind of love does not arise from the natural impulse to life, which you share with the rest of animate things; it arises from something deeper, something noble, and to be truthful, from something divine. You love life because it is the most precious gift a human being can receive in her short existence in this world—oh yes—because it is the noblest expression of the divine light. But unlike many people who adore the divine light for expedient reasons, you adore it and you love it because it is adorable and lovable, because you see the divine in it, because you see the beauty, the creative power, and the wisdom of this divinity. You do not love it only because it is the highest living flame of the divine light but also because you have an indelible appetite for it. I tend to think that you are enamored of it! Yes, you are. You cannot deny what I say. Please, do not think that I am shaming you. I admit your deep respect for the divine! Indeed, I am envious of you because I know much, very much, about the divine, but my problem is that I cannot be the refined soul you are! Even your late wife, who loved you passionately, died with the belief that you were in love with another woman, not knowing that you are in love with the divine! People find it difficult to fall in love with a man or a woman, and those who can achieve this kind of love are rare, as you know; but goodness, you are in love with the divine, with the beauty that transcends all finite beauty, the goodness that transcends all finite goodness, and the truth that transcends all finite truth.

"You must be a magician, not a trickster-magician who entertains people for a fee but the kind that descends from the heavens, from the bosom of the divine like a flaming meteorite of love. And yet everything about you and your life is *human, fully human.* You did not fall in love with the divine because of some freaky revelation, because you are a megalomanic, or because some sage deemed it a worthwhile ideal—oh, no! You love the divine because you love the world, and you love the world because it is an emanation from the divine light. How did you fall in love with the divine? Or how can the world exist if light does not shine in and through it? Again, tell me, how did you discover the divine in the world? Can the world exist in the dark? No, you did not discern light merely in the amazing scheme of nature, whose design dazzles the human mind with its magnificence, mystery, and beauty, and you did not discern it merely in the light that illumines it, but more clearly, more abundantly, more comprehensively in the striking design and powers of human nature—the human as such! And this discernment did not originate merely from reflection on the achievements of human beings in the course of human history during the past six millennia, which reveal the nature and magic of these powers, but especially from the love that shines in your heart, from your endeavor to cultivate the young in the art of thinking logically, morally, historically, aesthetically, and metaphysically, from the need to respond to the creator of this universe reverently. The countless students who recognize you as their spiritual father and who now assume high positions of leadership in the different institutions and organizations of the nation stand as a living testimony to the spark of love in your heart. Can anyone be a cultivator of human individuality, of nourishing the mind of the youth in the art of human living, if she does not love humanity?

"You were an outstanding example of creating and giving: the more you created, the more you produced, and the more you gave, the more you produced, the more you grew in the art of loving. Although you were not a conformist, and although your life emanated from your mind and will, you lived in harmony with everyone around you. You were a model of judicious judgment and individual integrity. But what is amazing, perhaps unbelievable, is that you lived philosophically. You did not only create your philosophy; you practiced it. Most if not all of the philosophers here and in other parts of the world pursue philosophy in their writing as well as in their teaching as a profession or as a career, but not you. You pursued it as *vocation*, as a way of life, as a way of being in the world, if you allow me to use your words. You grew as an individual the more your philosophy grew in depth. You never followed this or that philosopher, you never plagiarized, and you never joined a certain philosophy or philosophical movement, although your mind was and remains a story of the history of philosophy. Your eyes do not merely see the appearance of things; they see the essence that shines through the appearance. Is there a question, a type of reality, finite or infinite, you did not reflect on? No, I have read your books. They are a mirror of the essential structure of the world. Serious philosophers would agree with me that this mirror in fact reflects your comprehension of this very structure.

"But the only phenomenon that intrigues my mind and the mind of every thoughtful human being, and that you did not elaborate in detail, is the *phenomenon of death*. What is death? From the standpoint of ordinary experience, you are now in the last station of your life. Although you are reclining in your bed, you are in fact standing on the Edge with one foot in the realm of being and the other foot in the realm of nonbeing. As I asked earlier, do you really want to die?

"Please, don't try to interrupt me, Dr. Adams! I know you are restless! I beg you to be patient with me. Can anyone be a genuine artist of the human mind if she is not a lover of humanity? You are an artist of the human mind! But how can you be such an artist if you do not know the secret of the human spark? What is this secret? Can you reveal it? How did you find your way into the secret of the human heart and mind? How does the mind exist as a source, as a creative power, as a subject that designs a human life and realizes it?

"What does it mean to die? I have a strong feeling that you have reflected on this question. Unlike any other reality, regardless of whether it is human or natural, this phenomenon that people call 'death' does not seem to be a fact or something people can experience the way they experience rocks, lions, and mountains. It does not seem to be an object of reflection— am I right? But if it is not an object of reflection, how can we talk about it? Philosophers have written about it, artists have depicted it in a myriad of images, ordinary people created myths about it, and teachers discussed it—how? Please tell me, can we speak about it sensibly if it cannot be an object of reflection? We know one of its features—that people pass away. What is this 'passing away'? I know what it means for an object to be alive, but can I know what it means for a human being to die, or to be dead? Can I imagine, much less conceive, my own nonexistence? How can I leap into the sea of nonexistence and watch myself passing away? Oh!" the stranger exclaimed and added, "I speak to you as if I am a human being, but as you shall soon discover, I am not. I adopt the human way of talking only to make a conversation between us possible."

The stranger paused and then resumed his speech with a greater enthusiasm. "Oh, Dr. Adams, you are a towering human being. You are a rare person in these days just as your Socrates was rare in his society a long time ago. No human being with human eyes, regardless of whether he or she is small or big, good or bad, wise or fool, can stand unmoved by the radiance of your being! Do not think that I am trying to fawn over you to make you do me some kind of favor, because there is no need for me to indulge in this kind of human nonsense. I say the truth the way I see it. This is how I was created. You can say that it is my nature to say the truth the way I see it. Can your eyes falsify what they see? Your mind can falsify what they see, but your eyes cannot!

"I am here in this room to have a conversation with the man who probed the structure of the cosmic process as a whole and in the fullness of its details. Now I would like to see how this man *feels, thinks, and acts when he stands at the door of the land of nonbeing.*

"Yes, Dr. Adams, you lived a good life. You loved the world, and the world welcomed you with open arms; you loved teaching, and your students esteemed you; you loved to write, and the philosophical community appreciated your contribution to philosophical understanding; you loved Webster College, and your colleagues honored you. Many people would say that you are a fortunate human being, one blessed by the gods—"

At this point of the stranger's speech, Dr. Seneca Adams's brow began to contract into a thick frown, his right shoulder jerked a little, and his lips curled inward. He fixed a sharp look at this mysterious and rather aggressive stranger. He felt a strong desire to interrupt him, but for some inexplicable reason, he did not. Maybe he could not. He simply kept looking at him with puzzled eyes and obvious displeasure. It must have seemed to him that this man, this human anomaly, had suddenly descended from nowhere into his presence and without permission and had begun to ask him questions about the meaning of life and death. What was alarming, indeed frightening, to Dr. Adams was that the stranger seemed to know about him, his ideas, and his life. Who would feel calm, self-composed, or silent in the presence of such an anomaly? No one would blame Dr. Adams for feeling perturbed, if not angry. Nevertheless, the stranger noticed this sudden change in how his host was feeling and thinking, and he understood its meaning, but he did not allow Dr. Adams to interrupt him.

"Please, be patient with me, Dr. Adams. I know you have always shied away from any kind of praise, although you deserve it more than any professor in your college. I also know that you may be tired and need some rest. A little patience is all I need. But do I deserve it? What right do I have to barge into the privacy of your presence in this rude, intrusive manner?" The stranger paused for a moment, cast a thoughtful glance at Dr. Adams, and then added, "The only right I have to be here, and at this awkward moment of your life, if I have any right to pay you this extraordinary visit, is the right to hope—to hope that your courtesy will incline you more to pardon me and accept my presence than to admonish me and refuse to communicate with me. Your mind is a deep well of generosity, but if for some reason you do not allow me to drink from it, I shall appeal to the kindness of your heart. Can you deprive me of the goodness of your heart?"

But Dr. Adams did not have to respond to the stranger's plea because a nurse suddenly entered the room with two paper cups containing two pills. She approached the bed. "It is time for your medication, Dr. Adams," she said and then threw a curious look at the visitor who was standing at the foot of the bed.

The stranger was a tall, handsome young man. He was dressed in a black suit, white shirt, and red tie. His eyes, which were black, were covered with two thick black eyebrows. His cheeks were separated by a big aquiline nose that stood as a granite rock in the middle of his face. It seemed to the nurse that his eyes, which converged upon her the moment she appeared in the room, looked more like cameras than two human eyes, as if they were designed to scan everything that appeared within their purview. She felt as if those two cameras did not photograph her face but the feelings and ideas that lurked by it. *Who is this man?* she thought in the silence of her mind. *He does not look like a teacher, a student, or a friend. Why is he here in this room?* But the eyes of this stranger were penetrating; they were misanthropic. She was repulsed by him. She turned her eyes away from him and focused on Dr. Adams's kind face. To the stranger, she was a moving fixture in the room—no more than a fixture.

However, the nurse, who radiated warmth, felt the iciness of the stranger's look. She knew Dr. Adams, she knew the kind man he was, and she felt privileged to nurse him; but she could not understand how he would entertain a man made of ice, and she wondered whether a man like him should be allowed in the room. Nevertheless, she was a nurse, and she acted as one. She proceeded to the bed. "How do you feel now, Dr. Adams?"

"I am fine, Janice," he said in a rather subdued voice. She gave him the first pill, which he swallowed with a sip of water. He then breathed heavily and looked at her with a soft smile on his lips. She felt good! She, too, smiled and then gave him the second pill. The first pill was a strong painkiller, and the second was for blood pressure.

"A nap will make you feel better," she said and then added, "Do you need anything? Please do not hesitate, Dr. Adams!"

"No, my dear!"

"Do not hesitate, please; just press the red button if you need me." Dr. Adams smiled with a soft nod.

The nurse asked the same question twice, although differently, only because she did not feel comfortable with the visitor and to assure him that Dr. Adams's well-being was her top priority. The stranger stood at the foot of the bed more as a spectator than as a family member or friend. His icy complexion, especially his eyes, sent shivers of uneasiness into her mind. Janice had not been in the habit of judging people, and although she refrained from judging this visitor, she could not block a stream of negative vibes streaming from his appearance into her veins. She entertained the idea as she was tidying Dr. Adams's bed that he might be a friend, at least a decent human being, but this remained an idea. As long as ideas, even feelings, remain in one's mind, they do not inflict harm on other people. Nevertheless, she was willing to change her view of this man if his future conduct justified the need for it.

"I am not a foolish judge of character," the stranger said after Janice left the room. "She thinks that you are an angel and I am a monster, but I am not interested in how she or anyone else thinks of me because I know who I am and what I do. Now I am interested in you and in no one else—"

"In me? Why? *Who are you? Why are you here?*" Dr. Adams blurted out and fixed a solid stare into the stranger's face, expecting an answer to his questions.

"Why am I here?" the stranger wondered with a shade of surprise in his voice. "You should know why I am here!"

"No, I do not know who you are or why you are here. How can I guess why you are here if I do not know who you are? Who are you? You seem to know much about me, yet I do not remember meeting you as a former student, colleague, or philosopher."

"Is there a need to know my identity?"

"Certainly! How can you have a meaningful conversation or any kind of human interchange with a person you do not know? Besides, you do not seem to be interested in a conversation or enlightenment. You have intruded into my presence from nowhere; and you have been praising me as a philosopher, person, and teacher; and you have been talking about death in general and my imminent death in particular. You are a shrewd speaker, a flatterer, and an impertinent person. Even if I am a kind and generous person and a deep well of wisdom, as you say, does this justify your intrusion into my privacy? Would a person with a good heart violate the privacy of a human being consciously, knowingly, and voluntarily? The real question is whether your intrusion is justifiable regardless of whether I am kind, generous, or wise. My generosity or kindness may incline me to pardon your intrusion into my privacy, but it does not justify the imposition of your presence and lectures that you call conversation.

"Moreover, I can forgive a misdeed if the deed originates from a good heart or from ignorance, but did your intrusion originate from a good heart or from ignorance? I doubt it! Nothing about you inspires trust. The fact that you gave yourself the right to inquire about me and obtrude into my privacy implies that you consider yourself above any moral or rational norm, which inclines me to ask once more, who are you?"

"You are truly the illustrious Dr. Adams I know you are. Your intuition is sound—"

"I do not seek flattery, sir!" Dr. Adams said, interrupting the stranger. "I know who I am, and I know my strengths and limitations. Furthermore, I know that I am in the last station of my life. I just wish to know who you are!"

The stranger allowed a condescending grin to settle in the corner of his month. This grin remained in its place for a few seconds as his eyes were scrutinizing Dr. Adams's face. Then he said:

"I am Master Death!"

"Master who?" Dr. Adams said with a sarcastic tone in his rhetorical response.

"You heard me, Dr. Adams! I am Master Death."

Dr. Adams threw an unbelieving look at the stranger. "Is this your title or your name, the same name your parents gave you when you were born?"

"No, I do not have parents, and I was not born. No one gave me my name, Master Death, which functions as my name as well as my title, and which expresses my essence. I am my essence, and my essence is death. I was created simultaneously with the creation of the world. Unlike the objects that make up the structure of the universe, I have supernatural powers. I can assume any human or natural identity I choose. But although I have supernatural powers, I can neither interfere in nor violate the laws of nature. They were created by the same power that created me and the universe. Every object in the universe acts according to its essence or the purpose for which it was created. I have a purpose, and I have powers appropriate to my essence. In whatever I do, I cannot deviate from the pursuit of my purpose. I have no desire for truth, beauty, or love the way you do. Nothing you or anyone else does interests me. You may wonder why. The answer is simple. I have neither desires nor emotions; therefore, I cannot feel. How can I be curious if I do not have a faculty of desire, and how can I desire if I do not have a faculty of feeling? I am Master Death and nothing else. Therefore, I cannot meddle in the existence of the activities that happen around me.

"I have supernatural powers because I am pure power. The logic that governs my existence, my purpose, and the activities I perform in the human world is the logic of destruction, or extinction, but not the extinction of natural objects. I am the power that oversees the extinction of human beings. Natural objects do not die; they pass away."

This smorgasbord of ideas moved into Dr. Adams's mind with difficulty. He was a rational person: He thought, acted, and lived rationally. He always believed that an essential feature of reason or any rational activity is order. Therefore, a conversation or any meaningful discourse was, for him, a kind of rational order. However, contrary to his expectation, the stranger did present his ideas in an acceptable rational order. Dr. Adams felt a compelling desire to discuss the ideas and questions the stranger presented according to their conceptual and logical priority. Accordingly, the first question in need of clarification was his identity.

"When you claim that you are Master Death," Dr. Adams began, "you mean that 'Master Death' is neither your name nor your title but an expression of your essence, in the sense that you, the person who is now standing at the foot of my bed, are an ontic embodiment of a reality called death. In making this assertion, you assume that death is a reality and that you are a concrete embodiment of this reality. Accordingly, the proposition you are stating is that death exists. It follows from what you say that death is a kind of reality about which we can discourse rationally the way we discourse rationally about plants, animal, and rocks. In your earlier speech, you acknowledged that the death of human beings is not a public event or phenomenon. We do not experience it the way we experience natural or human phenomena, which implies that although it is a subjective reality, although it is a nonpublic event, nevertheless it is a reality no less real than the reality of the objects that make up the structure of the universe—do I understand you correctly?"

"Yes, you do, Dr. Adams," the stranger said with a grave expression of his face.

"Would you then agree that you have made two claims: first, death exists, and second, you are its embodiment? Accordingly, if death is not real, you would not be real—correct?"

"Correct," the stranger said with the same grave expression on his face.

"I shall not now examine the veracity of your twofold claim that death exists and that you are real, which I shall do in the proper context. But now let me express a feeling. Your claim that you are an embodiment of a reality you call death is intriguing, if not dubious—"

"Dubious?" the stranger snapped with a touch of anger in his voice.

"I was generous when I characterized it as intriguing and accurate when I characterized it as dubious."

The stranger thrust the wildest look you could imagine at Dr. Adams's' face. "What is the basis of your charge that I am an embodiment of death am dubious?"

"If you are an embodiment of death, in what sense are you death? Does death look like a human being? How can extinction, or the annihilation of a human being, assume or become transfigured into the human form I am now facing? Suppose you are Master Death; do you scare the people who fear death? How would they know that you are the source of their fear? Do they see you or in any way encounter you? But what is troublesome about your claim is this: the assertion that you are an embodiment of death implies that death is a reality and that you are its embodiment. What kind of reality do you embody?"

"I do not embody death the way an artwork embodies aesthetic qualities or beauty; I am a concretization of death itself," the stranger said.

"Again, "Dr. Adams asked, "if you are a concretization, what are you a concretization of? As you can see, I am inquiring about the stuff out of which you are a concretization. If what I am now seeing is not a human being, what do I see?"

"What you see is a flare of power—nothingness. For example, as this power I can, as I mentioned earlier, appear and disappear, and I can assume any form or identity I choose."

"What kind of power are you?"

"The kind that destroys."

"A power of destruction?"

"Yes, the essence of destruction is the annihilation or extinction of existing objects. I eliminate them from the realm of existence. The king of change is in charge of the annihilation of natural objects; I am in charge of the annihilation of human objects.

"Most people cannot think abstractly; they cannot conceive the existence of annihilation as an active productive power in the infinity of the realm of being. This power is real; it is influential the way any reality is influential. This is why it reveals itself to human beings as a concretization, one that not only embodies but is also the actuality of this power: this power is I, Master Death. Tell me, how would many people who pretend to be Christian believe in the existence of an infinite being, a being they cannot directly experience, conceive of, even understand, if that shrewd disciple of Jesus John had not fabricated the outlandish myth that God is a kind of logos and that Jesus Christ is an embodiment of this logos, so that the infinite becomes finite and the finite infinite, that God is Jesus and Jesus is God? But unlike the Christian logos, I am not ineffable or infinite; I am more real than the reality of the objects you see around you. Who can deny the existence of death? The young people cannot answer this question because they have not yet developed the eyes by which they can see or the mind that can comprehend it. But older people who have developed these eyes see it and dread it. They will not believe that I am Master Death not because they know I am he when they see me but because they are afraid of me or afraid to acknowledge my existence. I am their greatest enemy."

"If, as you say, you respect the laws of nature, and this respect stems from the fact that this is the way you were created, if you do not meddle in the lives of people; if, according to you, people are parts of nature and so subject to its laws in what they think, feel, and act; and if you cannot choose to kill them, what is your function as Master Death—just to watch people die?"

"First," Master Death said, "yes, I watch people die, and I delight in their death. I hate those mushy, so-called religious faithful, those weaklings who believe that they have a soul and that their soul is immortal. These people hate death, which means they hate me. They love to live forever, even though most of them do not deserve the short life they have on this earth. They are parasites on real life. They are worthless beggars. What gratifies me is that they are wrong, delusive. I do my best to ensure their eternal death."

"How?"

"By promoting their ignorance."

"You seem to be vengeful."

"I am not vengeful; I am rightful."

"How do you apply your rightfulness if you are right?"

"Have you ever observed how those weaklings live? Publicly they look cheerful, happy, successful, courageous, wise, confident, and most of all self-righteous, but in the privacy of their minds and hearts, they live a life of dismal anxiety, spiritual poverty, fear, and self-deception, a life that verges on comical neurosis. Their instinct, which is stronger than their reason, tells them that they do not have a soul, that they will die the way plants and animals die, and that all their achievements, which are worthless anyway, and all their vainglory will end up in the land of nothing! Watch how they cover up the reality of their impending death. I shall not consider the methods they use to cover it up now, but they cover it out of fear, yes, out of fear, not of death but of human life, of living up to the highest promise of their humanity. I am the source of their fear. What is human life but a life of creative action, of pursuing the ideals that spring from the essential needs of human nature? I am rightful by transforming their life into a living hell.

"How can you consider yourself living if you do not ground your personal life, its principles and values, in the light that illuminates the universe? Didn't you teach this fundamental precept to your students, Dr. Adams? Yes, you did! But unfortunately, most of your fellow human beings lead a life of the herd, not the life of the shepherd, not the life of a human community, one composed of *human individuals*. The human individual is a shepherd of her life. The human community is a community of human shepherds. I do not deny that the human herd are human beings in the sense that they possess the essence of humanity, that is, the capacities of thinking, feeling, willing, and creating, and I do not deny that they use these faculties in meeting their daily needs; what I am saying is that they use them as a means of basic survival. They are satisfied with a few crumbs of human satisfaction. They do not use them as a means of *human survival—*"

"What do you mean by 'human survival'?" Dr. Adams asked, interrupting the stranger.

"Human survival is the survival of the human being *as a human being.*"

"This answer is painfully vague. Can you explain how a human being survives as a human being?"

"Yes," the stranger said. "The essence, or that which makes people human and distinguishes them from the rest of natural objects, consists of capacities, each one of which is a power. They are the capacities of thinking, feeling, willing, and creating. Reason is the capacity by which people seek knowledge and understanding; feeling is the capacity by which they seek and enjoy important things; willing is the capacity by which they meet their personal needs and become the individuals they should be; and creating is the capacity by which they actualize their vocation in life. The first capacity aims at the value of truth or wisdom; the second aims at the values of beauty and goodness; the third aims at the value of freedom; and the fourth aims at the value of human perfection, sometimes known as human growth and development. Broadly speaking, creativity is a necessary condition for seeking and realizing any meaningful action or project in human life because these four capacities do not exist as ready-made faculties;

they exist in human nature as potentialities awaiting realization. People are not born as thinkers, lovers of beauty and goodness, free, or farmers, engineers, or teachers, but with the power to become thinkers, lovers of beauty and goodness, free, and teachers, engineers, or farmers. The realization of human potentiality is essentially a creative activity because the basic human skills—for example, thinking or loving—emerge in the process of education; they come into being in this very process. I here assume that the sphere of education is not restricted to the school but includes the family, the workplace, the social context, and of course personal experience.

"As potentialities, the four capacities are infinite possibilities of realization. Is there a limit to how much a person can know, love, appreciate beauty, or grow as a human individual? Since the human essence exists as a potentiality, it would be reasonable to say that a person is a human being inasmuch as she realizes the capacities that define her humanity. Accordingly, the question is not whether people possess the human essence as a potentiality or whether they walk on two feet, but whether they realize this essence in the process of human living. One survives as a human being inasmuch as she grows in human perfection. Growth in this kind of perfection is the substance of human survival!

"Now"—the stranger paused and then continued—"cast an investigative look at the people who populate planet Earth and then tell me how many of them lead a creative way of life, that is, a life of human growth and development! Ironically, people everywhere in the world are being transformed into a kind of herd. The *human individual*, about whom you have been lecturing all your life, is increasingly becoming an abstraction that inhabits the minds of idealists and dreamers only. On the ground of reality, people are enmeshed in an unusually complex social, political, economic, and cultural web that is most of the time governed by leaders who are hungry for wealth, power, and glory, not by a genuine desire to transform the different societies of the world into human communities, communities in which people live according the values that reflect the essential demands of human nature. The various institutions and organizations that constitute the structure of this web are gradually becoming autocratic if not despotic. Everywhere people thrive within a highly sophisticated system of rules, norms, national policies, social expectations. This system is gradually becoming a kind of straitjacket. How can one move intellectually, professionally, morally, politically, and especially creatively, or how can one become the individual she should be in this kind of straitjacket? Let me shed more light on this point. I ask you to be patient in the way I present my ideas to you." Dr. Adams did not respond to the stranger, but he gave him a nod of approval.

"The concept of death implies passing away, but not every case of passing away is necessarily a case of death. Natural objects do not die; they pass away. They come into being and they pass out of being, but they do not die. Death is a peculiar aspect of humanity. Death is more, much more than the event of passing away. The source and basis of human beings' death is knowledge, and the basis of this knowledge is self-consciousness. Unlike natural objects, human beings do not merely pass away; they also know what it means for them to pass away, and they know what it means for them to pass away as human beings. Regardless of whether they are rocks, plants, or animals, natural objects do not know what it means for them to pass away. In a chase of a flock of deer by a hunter, if one deer breaks its leg and falls to the ground, the flock does not wait for it, they do not carry it on their backs, and they do not remain by its side; on the contrary, they look at it for a few seconds and then continue their run, as if they had not lost one of their companions.

"Moreover, natural objects exist and endure according to the laws of nature: they do not create themselves, and they do not control their lives. They do not have what some of your colleagues call 'subjectivity' or privacy. They do not ask questions, and they do not wonder about the meaning of their lives or about existence in general. But human beings are not merely natural objects; they are also human objects. They are given to the world as natural objects but with the potentiality of becoming human beings. If this potentiality is not realized, they exist and live as members of the animal world, not in the human world. Human beings are capable of creating themselves as human individuals, as individuals in charge of their lives. They cannot create their bodies or their human essence, but they can create themselves as human individuals! Accordingly, the human individual is a personal achievement. This individual is a world. The question that merits special consideration now is, what does it mean for this individual, this world, to die? The focus in raising this question is not on the death of human beings in general but the death of the particular human being, this very human being that is a private world. *This is a personal, not a general question because the event of death is an absolutely private event!* One knows what it means for her to die, but she cannot know what it means for the other person to die. Even the individual cannot fully grasp what it means for her to die because the event of death is a one-time event and experience. It is incomparable because the individual dies before she can understand it or compare it.

"But what is strange, and for me amusing, is that most of the people around you do not die as human beings. Those who really die are few, very few. They are truly developed as human beings—like you, Dr. Adams. How can one die as a human being if she does not live as a human being? Has it occurred to you that only those who strive to live as human individuals, those whose lives are living sparks of human self-realization, are not afraid of death—of me? I loathe those people. They are my supreme challenge, and they are my adversaries. They are strong and hard to subjugate to my will. The secret of their strength is knowledge. I am sure that they know more than anyone around you that knowledge is a source not only of light, of understanding, but also of strength, of courage, of patience, of hope, of caring, even of cunning, not the cunning of the foxes but of the creative impulse of human nature, of the noble genius—of the gods who patronize art, science, philosophy, technology. Your illustrious Renaissance philosopher Francis Bacon realized that knowledge is power and that it is the primary kind of power by which human beings can appropriate nature to their ends. I am a different kind of power. I am the kind that inhibits the growth and development of humanity. You preach the gospel of love, justice, freedom, and creation; I preach the gospel of hate, indolence, selfishness, discord, bondage, and destruction. Humanity is a crystal palace, a place where human beings flourish. Human values cannot thrive in a world of hate, indolence, discord, love, injustice, bondage, and destruction. I am Master Death, but metaphorically speaking, I am the god of darkness. As you know, the tree of human life cannot grow in the world of darkness."

Dr. Adams's patience with the stranger had been extinguished some time ago, and he was doing his best to find a way to free himself from this irrelevant academic jargon, most of which was boring to him. Luckily, Dr. Stanley Lawson, professor of physics, was already standing at the door of his room. It was clear to Dr. Adams that his visitor had heard the last part of the stranger's speech on the nature of death and his view of genuine human living, but Dr. Adams was very glad to see him, specially to take a seriously needed break from this uninvited visitor. "I can come later," Dr. Lawson said, still standing at the door of the room. His eyes met the stranger's eyes, but there was no communication between them. On the contrary, the stranger was vexed.

"There is no reason for you to leave, Dr. Lawson," and looking at Dr. Adams, the stranger added, "We shall continue this conversation."

Stanley Lawson was Dr. Adams's dear friend and confidant. He was a nuclear physicist, but he was deeply interested in cosmology. He was curious about the source, structure, and evolution of the universe as a creative process. He believed that an understanding of the source of this process was essential to an adequate conception of the nature of the things that come into being in this process, especially its purpose, if it has one. He had even collaborated with Dr. Adams on an interdisciplinary book titled *Principles of Cosmology*. Unlike Dr. Adams, who was a quiet and private person, Dr. Lawson was immersed in the communal life of the college. Although he was trained as a physicist and had made important contributions to our understanding of photons and electrons, practically he was first and foremost a cosmologist. His scientific mind was interdisciplinary, holistic. He thought that the knowledge advanced by the physicist was an integral part of the general of map of human knowledge. For him, some academicians had set some artificial boundaries between the different types of knowledge, but he believed that a seeker of knowledge in any area of human experience could not view these boundaries as rigid or final. One could not understand the nature of living organisms without an adequate understanding of the aims of physics, geology, and chemistry, and one could not understand the nature of human beings without an equally adequate understanding of the physical and natural sciences. The scientific mind, he once observed to his friend Dr. Adams, was essentially a cosmological mind, and the cosmological mind was essentially a metaphysical mind. The established scientific method did not necessarily exclude the philosophical method of thinking, and the knowledge achieved by the different sciences was indispensable to philosophical reflection and analysis.

Dr. Adams frequently invited his colleague to deliver lectures on the nature of the cosmic process and the extent to which one could infer the existence of a primary cause, or an *arche,* of this process. He emphasized to all his students that a serious comprehension of the dynamics of the cosmic process was critically relevant to our understanding of the meaning of existence in general and human existence in particular.

But the purpose of Dr. Lawson's visit to his friend that afternoon was neither academic nor personal. It was a case of moral abortion.

"Moral abortion?" Dr. Adams exclaimed after the two friends greeted each other and discussed the most recent development of Dr. Adams's illness.

"Yes, from my point of view, it is a case of moral abortion," Dr. Lawson said. "I never expected that the dean of the college is a racist."

"The dean?" Dr. Adams asked, his eyes emanating a wild surprise.

"Yes, unbelievable. The dean is the face of the college, of what it stands for. I shall not dwell on this point now. But please, tell me what happened."

"As you know, it is customary for the dean to invite the new faculty and their wives or husbands to dinner at his house at the beginning of the academic year. This is a way of welcoming them to the Webster community. We shall have six new faculty members this year. But only five were invited to the dean's house. The sixth member, Ramos Mitzakis, who has just received his terminal degree from the University of Wisconsin, was willing to teach in Mississippi—"

"He was willing? What do you mean?" Dr. Adams inquired, astonished.

"Yes, Dr. Brooks was unable to recruit any young or even older professors at the last American Philosophical Association conference—"

"Why?" Dr. Adams asked, interrupting Dr. Lawson.

"Again, why?" Dr. Adams asked.

"They are afraid to come. The civil rights riots seem to scare anyone in the nation to teach in Mississippi. We have a very bad reputation. Besides, they treat Mississippi as a backward state. Anyway, Ramos was excluded from that welcome dinner. He did not know about it or about this Webster tradition. Two days later, I asked how he and his wife enjoyed their dinner with the dean. 'What dinner?' he wondered, surprised. Mitzakis shook his head, twisted his lips inward, and then said, 'I was not invited.'

"'But you were supposed to be invited,' Dr. Brooks, current chair of the philosophy department, responded.

"'Maybe, but I was not invited.'

"'Brooks told me that he spoke with the dean's secretary, Mary, and asked her why Mitzakis had not been invited to the welcome dinner. She was silent for a few seconds, and in fact she was confused. Then she looked at him and said, 'As far as I know, Dr. Mitzakis's name was on the list of invited guests. I cannot explain why his name was removed from the list.'

"'Does the dean know?'

"'You should speak with him.'

"Dr. Brooks asked Mary to arrange a meeting with the dean, and the dean was able to see Brooks on the following afternoon. After they exchanged a few pleasantries, Brooks asked, 'Why was Mitzakis disinvited to the welcome dinner a few days ago?'

"This question fell upon the dean's face as a thunderbolt. His face suddenly blushed. His eyes widened. He tried to swallow his saliva, but there was no saliva to swallow. The dean was a heavy smoker; in fact, he was a chain-smoker. Involuntarily, his hand moved toward a cigarette packet and pulled out a cigarette with trembling fingers. He inhaled a whiff of smoke into his chest, threw an equally trembling look at Brooks's face, hesitated a little, and said, 'Disinviting Mitzakis was good for the college.' He paused for a second and then added, 'And for me.'

"'How?'

"'It is too early to allow foreigners, especially from the Middle East, to join the Webster community.'

"'But Mitzakis is a human being.'

"'I know he is. I just do not wish to be philosophical about it now.'

"'What if I remind you that he is a Christian and was educated at Union College, a Methodist institution, under the tutorship of a Methodist minister?'

"'It does not matter. He is different. He is a foreigner, and he is from the Middle East. His native tongue is Arabic. This is all I can say to you.' With the same trembling hands, the dean took in a deep whiff from his cigarette, held it in for a second, and then let the smoke leave his esophagus slowly; he watched the smoke thoughtfully, as if he were looking for some intuition or inspiration from the cloud of smoke he had created.

"It seemed to Brooks that the dean had received a bout of courage from that cloud, for he pierced a sharp look at him and with a soft nod said, 'As a philosopher, you should know that welcoming foreigners into our community is not merely a matter of following institutional, moral, and social norms and practices; it is also, and more importantly, an outlook, a matter of what we are and what we stand for in this world. What we are is determined by our values. These values did not fortuitously fall from the skies; they gradually evolved. They do not exist in some book or on some tablet; they permeate the mind, the psyche, of our institutional and social selves. You cannot change culture overnight by legislating a law or by a presidential decree. Culture is a human institution; it originates, grows, matures, and progresses or declines by the kind of spiritual, economic, and political circumstances it confronts and the projects it designs and implements. On the contrary, we do not receive them the way we receive ideas and gifts, or the way we receive food or water. We discover what we are when we grow and mature rationally and socially. We discover that we are Christians, Jews, Muslims, or Hindus; we discover that we are American, Chinese, Indian, French, or Spanish; and we discover that we have certain emotions, dispositions, habits—in short, ways of thinking and living. The material and spiritual conditions that nourish human character are an unusually intricate network of beliefs, values, and cultural forces. These are formidable facts; they are a kind of firm wall. It is futile to try to pull down this wall by one act, as you know.

"'I may strike you as a racist. Fine! Go ahead. View me as one. But I am not the only racist among the faculty. Most of them are racists. They act as if they are not, but underneath the surface they are. I am afraid that Mitzakis will have a very hard time. He may have to leave soon, or he may suffer to the end of time. I have already received negative reactions against him, especially from Merchant in my department. He could not see a foreigner as a member of our faculty. This Merchant pretends to be liberal, but he does not give a hoot about the truth or about human dignity. I am quite sure that he will do his best to discredit and most likely undermine Mitzakis. Only God knows what he will do. Nevertheless, you will be making a mistake if you oppose my decision.'

"'But what is wrong with inviting him to your home?'

"'Disinviting him was a symbolic gesture. It was my attempt to appease those who have strongly opposed his appointment. You are what you are, and you are able to converse with me about this critical issue because you are a member of this community. If you violate or in any way undermine the spirit of the community, you will by the same fact undermine the community and necessarily yourself as a faculty member. As a dean, I function as an official who respects the Webster community.

"'By the way, most of the faculty support the way I have acted in this case. I have a strong hunch that if you were in my position, you would act the way I did. As a dean, I do not make decisions on the basis of my personal feelings and ideas. I act as a servant of the college, as a servant of the interests of the college. This all I can say to you, Fred.'

"'Have you considered Mitzakis's feelings? We freely hired him. Do we have a right to treat him this way? We need him.'

"'He needs us more than we need him?'

"'We sought him. He had never heard of Webster College.'

"'He should be thankful to us for giving him a job—' the dean said.

"'Giving him a job as a member of the community?'

"'As an instructor,' the dean said.

"'Still,' Dr. Brooks pressed the dean, 'as a member of the community?'

"'He is not one of us.'

"'Can he become one of us?'

"'He is culturally, politically, socially different from us. Can you mix olive oil and water?'

"'How can we as Christians act in a non-Christian way?'

"'Is he more or less human than you or me? Isn't the Christian ideal the basis of the Webster way of life?'

"'This is not a religious issue; it is a cultural and practical issue. It is also a historical issue. How we now behave is the outcome of a long history. No one can change what history has done with a magical wand. You may condemn it, but you cannot try it in court of moral law. Can you? I tend to think that we should consider this question within the wider context of racism. The racist believes that racial differences are real and that some races are superior to others intellectually, physically, socially, and culturally; and some racists believe in the purity of their race, which is a strange piece of fiction. They view this purity as a sacrosanct value. If you believe you are superior to a certain person, you will tend to treat her as inferior. Logically, the inferior person would be subservient to the superior person. Cast a quick look at the way the ancient Greeks treated foreigners; how the Romans treated the Christians; how conquerors, which applies to the colonialists of the past and the present, treated the conquered people; how aristocrats treated serfs, slaves, and plebians; and how some Americans treated Black people. The eyes of the racist are blind to the fact, which was preached by the founders of the major religions of the world, that regardless of their differences, all human beings are equal in their humanity. Those eyes are also blind to the fact that the human essence is given to us as a potentiality, not as a fully realized individual nature. We are not born as aristocrats, teachers, farmers, artists, scientists, political leaders, or engineers, but with the potentiality to become any one of these. The realization of this potentiality takes place under certain economic, educational, political, religious, and cultural conditions. Change these conditions and you change the nature and direction of how the human potential is realized.'

"But then is this way of treating educated people by a college such as Webster consistent with the ideals of liberal education and the values of the church? Webster is supposed to be a Christian college. Moreover, it is supposed to be the leading liberal arts institution in the state.'

"'I beg you not to ask me any further questions!'

"I have rehearsed to you my conversation with Fred only to give you an idea of the logic Bandy used to justify his disinvitation of Mitzakis."

"I understand you, Stanley."

"This affair is scandalous, Seneca. But I think it will remain under the rug like many similar affairs."

"I wonder whether you can characterize it as scandalous. It is a way of life at Webster. Foreigners, native Indians, Blacks, or anyone who is not white or descended from a European origin will not be admitted into our community. Dr. Cochran, chair of the sociology department, thinks that recruiting white students only is a hidden policy of the college. It is a kind of fixture in the Webster administration. She questioned Mr. Brown, director of recruiting, when he gave his annual report about the new freshman class, asking him to explain why we do not have black or nonelite students at the college. His answer was simple: 'We recruit the best high school graduates in the state.'

"'Do you recruit students in Black schools? Are there no qualified black high school graduates?' The director evaded the question. There was a very faint hum among the faculty."

"But then why did the dean hire Mitzakis?" Dr. Adams asked.

"Because he had no choice. He approved Mitzakis's appointment for one year only. What is even worse is that his salary was not higher than the salary of a high school teacher."

"How did Mitzakis react to this kind of treatment, to this form of human degradation?"

"He did not react. He was in a bind; he was penniless. His wife gave birth to their first child a few months ago. He urgently needed some means of survival."

"It seems to me that the dean exploited Mitzakis."

"He certainly did, but the question is, why did he exploit him? How could a person in his position as a dean indulge in exploitation? I really wonder whether he felt any qualms about his action."

When he heard this question, Dr. Adams turned his face away from Dr. Lawson and succumbed to a sad, reflective gaze into the corner of the room. Something about this remark must have provoked a swarm of feelings and memories in his mind. Dr. Lawson understood the meaning of that look, but he was anxious to understand the dynamics that had produced it.

"You know the college, and you know the way it functions, more than any other faculty member," he said, freeing Dr. Adams from that sad gaze, "and as far as I know, I am a newcomer; this practice should not be tolerated, not at an institution such as Webster College. We prepare some of the most competent and influential leaders for the state. These leaders are supposed to embody the moral, social, religious values the college stands for. They should be living examples of the truly educated person. How can our students be such examples if we, the governors and faculty of the college, do not respect and promote these values not only in our teaching but also in our personal and professional behavior? Don't we indulge in a kind of academic, if not moral, hypocrisy when we behave in the way we behaved toward Mitzakis? Isn't our obligation to create an atmosphere in which the faculty, the staff, and the students acknowledge the supremacy of the values of the college? I have always thought that Webster should be a haven of learning, teaching, and living. How can this kind of place exist, much less thrive, if its leaders do not act in the light of these values?" Dr. Lawson said and then looked into his friend's eyes and added, "Am I a foolish dreamer?"

"No—" Dr. Adams tried to respond to his friend's remarks, but he could not because a ball of severe pain was raging wildly and frantically in his right lung. It was so severe, it almost choked him. Reflexively, he pressed the red button on the handset that was hanging at the side of the bed. He threw an apologetic look at his friend and murmured, "Patience!" He paused for a second and continued with the same murmuring voice. "Please!"

Dr. Lawson left his chair instantly and was about to dash to the nurses' station, but he did not only because Janice was practically running toward the room. One glance at her patient was all she needed to know what he was feeling. In fact, he was not merely feeling unbearable pain; he was also trembling. Janice left the room without uttering a word and returned in less than a minute with a syringe in her hand. She injected Dr. Adams's right arm with a dose of painkiller.

"He should feel better momentarily," she said when her eyes met Dr. Lawson's eyes. She adjusted the pillow that supported Dr. Adams's back and stood next to Dr. Lawson. Both of them gaped into their patient's face.

Although fire burns, and when it is torrid and consumes the victim who suffers the pangs of its ruthless teeth, Dr. Adams was self-composed during that attack. The only language, perhaps expression, that revealed the intensity of the pain was his trembling body, which he could not control. Pain is not only a staunch enemy; it is also an adversary, and it is an adversary because it is a challenge that threatens one's courage, capacity for feeling, hope, the instinct of survival, even love of life. Pain is a dark cloud that surges into a person's consciousness from the abyss of nonbeing. It weakens her rational vision, jumbles her emotions, and rocks her will. Pain is the kind of hammer that aims at the joints that hold the frame of the structure of the human self together, at the tendons that underlie the unity of that structure, and rips it into shreds. Have you ever been a victim of such pain, dear reader? Dr. Adams was in the throes of such pain when he was having a conversation with his dear friend. It is, I think, important to remark that the only way Dr. Lawson knew to console his friend was to engage him in a conversation, which Dr. Adams valued very much. A conversation activates the vital powers of the mind, but more importantly, it is one of the highest modes of human being, of being with the person we love. You do not console a human being truly with flowers or chocolate or with vacuous clichés of endearment and good wishes. You console her by your human presence, which is your most important possession. A meaningful conversation is one of the most important means of creating this kind of presence primarily because it consists of sharing your intellect, your heart, and your will, because as a human being you exist in the medium of this kind of presence. A meaningful conversation is an event of human loving.

On the following morning, Dr. Lawson was sitting on a wooden chair next to his friend's bed when Dr. Adams opened his eyes to the world. The warmth of his friend's presence attracted his attention. Human warmth is a kind of language the human heart understands more adequately than any other type of language. This kind of warmth reached Dr. Adams's heart as a morning greeting. He simply smiled and said, "Good morning, Stanley!"

"And to you, Seneca. How is your sleep these days?"

"My sleep?" He repeated the question with a friendly but cynical smile on his lips. "It is usually peaceful when they give those potent drugs; otherwise, it is tortuous, depressing."

"How?"

"I read in a number of serious books that when a human being lives a good life, when she intends the good in everything she does, when she seeks the true, the good, and the beautiful, she would feel inner peace when she reaches the last station of her life."

"Maybe! But I seem to be an exception," Dr. Adams said.

"Why? As far as I know, yours has been an admirable example of the good life—by any standard you try to evaluate it. I do not see why you should be an exception."

"I doubt that I am such an example. The only thing I do not doubt is that I tried to be one. But regardless of one's intention or whether we succeed in leading a life of goodness, the course of human life in general is never smooth; on the contrary, it is a continual ascent of a mountain of challenges, temptations, obstacles, and ignorance that frustrates the completion of one's life project. There are no final rules, dicta, or even gems of wisdom that guide one's way into the future. Leading a life of goodness is not different from creating a beautiful statue out of a slab of marble. The sculptor does not know what the statue will be like until she completes her work. If she knew what it would look like, she would not be an artist because then there would be no need to create it."

"I see the point you are trying to make. Still, I would like to know about your dreams."

"Nightmares! During the night I am caught between two crushing hammers, deadening silence produced by the potent drugs, which knock me out of existence, and the spiteful nightmares that knock me out of my wits."

"Are these nightmares caused by the drugs?"

"Some people would attribute them to the drugs they take, and in some cases, drugs can be their cause, but I have a different view."

"What is it?" Dr. Lawson was quick to ask.

"When the Edge, the final stop of your life, stares you in the eyes shamelessly, your sense of time changes. Your mind undergoes a radical shift of focus. When you are young, you practically live in the future. Your future is a kind of endless vista of being; it is an arena in which you plan what you need to do or desire the next day, week, month, and maybe year. The future is the basis of what you do and how you live. When you are a child, you envision and in some cases you long to be in high school, and when you are in high school, you long, if you are interested, to be in college, and when you are in college, you long to find a job and get married. When you get married and find a job, you long to be successful in your profession, thinking that success is the key to the happiness the world promised you when you were born. This process is rather sketchy. I mention it only to emphasize that the life of the human individual is a plan, regardless of whether it is designed foolishly or wisely, consciously or by the circumstance of your life, and that the realization of this plan is always unfolding in the future. In a way, the future we plan is the present in which we live. For example, when I think of what I shall do tomorrow, doesn't tomorrow become my present? This plan and the determination to pursue it transform my tomorrow and my today into a continuum. The future collapses into the present, and the present collapses into the future.

"But when you reach the station that overlooks the Edge of your life, when your eyes fail to see a future when you cannot make any future plans or have any serious expectations, which means you cannot live in or for the future. You are stuck with and in the past. Your future contracts. You cannot any longer plan for more than a few years. If you happen to be healthy, you can envision the possibility of a few years that some people call retirement, as if this term signifies retirement from life and not merely from the routine work. But those few years tend to pass quickly, more quickly than they did when you were young. If you happen to be sick, if you know that your days are few, you mostly live in the past because this is all you have. You feel that your past is a kind of corner, and you feel that you are stuck in it. What can you do in such a corner? But alas, you are your past: your past life is summed up, condensed in your present, in the being you now are. During the day you are forced to remember something that happened in the past during your childhood, adolescence, middle age, or old age. Usually what you remember is something important, regardless of whether it is good or bad, ugly or beautiful, glorious or inglorious. Speaking metaphorically, the past stands before your eyes as a kaleidoscopic movie. Sometimes it reveals events you have forgotten or you do not wish to remember, but most of the time you remember the painful events; indeed, these events force themselves into your present consciousness. These events include the big mistakes you committed, the bad deeds you performed, the injustices inflicted upon you, the blunders you caused because of ignorance, and the calamities caused by bodily and psychological infirmities. You were able to suppress these and similar painful events by planning certain projects or by performing this or that task or by indulging in this or that pleasure. But now you do not and cannot have any serious plans, and you cannot indulge in serious pleasure. You become a problem to yourself: how should I live decently now—in the remainder of my life?

"During the day, you have two options: you either dwell on your past, which is not rewarding, or indulge in some method of killing time by watching movies, reading books, chatting with your friends, travelling to this or that interesting place, or listening to music, not because you choose to perform any of these activities but because you have no choice. In some cases, people pursue constructive, productive courses of action by donating their knowledge, talent, or possessions to worthwhile projects and organizations, but this is not possible in my case. You try to pass the time left for you, and you try to justify whatever you do to the best of your ability. But no matter what you do, an underlying consciousness constantly sneaks into what you are doing at the present. Although this consciousness raises many questions and feelings, two feelings stand out. The first is a feeling of guilt about the mistakes you committed and the injustices inflicted upon you by nature and others. The second is the distinct, irresistible awareness that the world you have been constructing ever since the moment you became conscious of your existence will soon sink in the ocean of nonbeing. No rational or sane human being can either ignore or suppress this awareness. What is even worse, your new eyes, the eyes time opened up in your mind, begin to see, albeit from a distance, the darkness that awaits you. If you happen to have achieved worthwhile works, you cannot but ask, Will these too sink into that ocean? Why?

"I am not raising these questions and making these observations because I feel either guilty or afraid of this destiny but because it is a human imperative to acknowledge that this kind of destiny is an important element of the human condition in this life. The ancients believed that human beings were playthings in the hands of their gods; we can now say that human beings are playthings in the hands of Fate, or perhaps the Cosmic Process."

Dr. Adams was in need of a short break. His breast was heaving rather heavily. He looked into his friend's eyes and said, "When you grow old, Stanley, every faculty of your mind gets weaker, especially your memory—" But Dr. Adams could not continue this sentence because Janice came into the room with a cheerful smile on her face.

"How is my lovely patient today?" she said.

Dr. Adams did not answer this question directly. Dr. Lawson left his chair and went to the foot of the bed.

"I feel fine, but I think I shall need a painkiller in the next few minutes."

"How was your sleep last night?" Janice asked as she was tucking the wrinkled sheet of his bed. The sheets were not always wrinkled so fiercely. She stole a look at Dr. Lawson when she was adjusting the foot of the cover. Their eyes met. They understood each other.

"Rocky!" Dr. Adams said hesitantly.

"I shall fetch your blood pressure medicine and a painkiller as soon as you eat your breakfast. The attending doctor, Dr. Monroe, will see you later this morning."

Janice moved to the right side of the bed and held Dr. Adams's hand for a few seconds, pressed it softly, and embraced his face with the kindest, warmest, and purest look one could imagine. Her eyes began to tear. She checked the tears, but not for long because they rolled over her cheeks as she was leaving the room without uttering a word or making a gesture.

TWO

Liberal Arts Education

D r. Adams's bed was empty when Dr. Lawson came to see him the following morning. He knew that his friend was in pain, that his days were numbered, and that he was willing to prolong his living days only because he deemed human life sacred. Human life is a divine gift. This is why we cannot destroy it. He also knew that his visits were a source of joy to Dr. Adams, the kind of gift that makes one wish to love life and relish it a little longer! They were also the source of the hope, courage, strength one needs to bear pain during the night. I say "night" because Dr. Adams confessed to him one day that in many of his nightmares during the night, he would imagine himself standing next to his bed watching himself dying in a pool of brutal, seething, excruciating pain. He would tremble at the sight of himself roasting in the fire of that pain, and he would choke when he was experiencing himself collapsing in his bed in a fit of debilitating spasm, only to wake up suddenly and find himself in the throes of one of those ferocious spasms. His days and nights were practically continuous. Pain does not know the difference between night and day, yesterday and today, here and there. It is a flame of sizzling fire that transcends space and time.

Dr. Lawson was meditating on his friend's condition—on his suffering, on his courage, on his drive for the highest level of spiritual life, on his devotion to the well-being of other people, and especially on his capacity to remain a fountain of love in the middle of this fatal state of being. He was also meditating on the implications of his death for the life of the college. "Webster will not be the same without him," he wrote in his daily journal. "He has been its sage, its lighthouse, and the highest embodiment of its ideals—of what it means for the college to be a liberal arts institution. No major policy or change in the curriculum was designed or implemented, and no major problem was solved without his advice or approval, not because he was powerful but because he was a radiance of care, of understanding and wisdom. His students loved him, his colleagues respected him, and the dean dreaded him. Among the students he was known as the teacher, among his colleagues he was known as the scholar, and to the dean he was known as the philosopher. The students saw in him a caring, honest, and competent teacher; the faculty saw in him a curious, creative, and productive mind; and the dean saw in him a leader and a teacher. Almost every advisor in the different academic departments recommended to their advisees that they should take at least one course with Professor Adams before leaving the college. Dr. Weimer, head of the psychology department, said that no Webster student should graduate without taking a course with this distinguished teacher."

Seneca, Dr. Lawson reflected, *is not a traditional instructor.* He had once said to Dr. Haworth that "he is an artist. He does not deliver his lectures; he is his lectures. He lectures with his mouth, hands, face, legs, in short, with his body. His lectures emanate from his body. You do not merely hear what he says. Although you hear every word he says, you also see and feel and see what he says. His lectures do not flow only from his mind but also from his heart. How can you doubt the seriousness and integrity of such a teacher? How can you take him lightly? How can you leave his lecture room without wondering, without thinking about what he had said or tried to say? It Is very hard for the student to digress or to take a mental break from his lectures."

One day Dr. Adams confided to Dr. Lawson that "ideas—meaningful ideas, that is—are not dead or inert abstractions that move from the mind of the teacher to the mind of the student the way you move objects from one place to another; they are drops, flames of fire, of living meaning. The mind of the student is not a kind of box, nor is it a store of ideas. It is a quantum of creative power. Its essence is thinking, feeling, and willing. The task of the teacher is to inspire the student to think from within, to feel from within, and to will from within. When you engage her in the analysis or explanation of an idea or a problem, she thinks with you; she feels what she thinks. She does merely receive ideas into her mind as a kind of trust. The question is how you can empower the students to participate in an activity of thinking. This is the secret, and this is the miracle, of the educative process.

"The student is not interested in dormant ideas, in sleepy ideas; she is hungry for life, for ideas that enliven the mind. Meaning is the fire that enlivens the mind. The mind of the student loves this kind of fire! Unfortunately, most of the ideas that fly in the space of the lecture halls of our educational institutions are much of the time abstract, recondite, technical, irrelevant to the student at that period of her growth as a human individual. The most formidable challenge when I face my students in the classroom is how to translate, how to make understandable the complex or technical ideas to the student. Many of the ideas we teach are most of the time taken out of their historical and conceptual contexts. How can the student comprehend them in terms of that context? We should always remember that the student is usually ignorant of that context. This is a main reason why she is a student. How can you enable her mind to see the meaning of those ideas? Is it an accident that teaching has frequently been reduced to a process of transmitting ideas, and learning to a process of storing them in the mind of the student—for a short period?! This twofold process stifles the mind of the student. It prevents it from thinking analytically and creatively. But the point of teaching and learning is to enable the student to think analytically, critically, and creatively. What is learning if it is not growth in the art of thinking and creating, and what is teaching if it is not an activity of cultivating this art? The student will sooner or later forget most if not all of the ideas she was asked to memorize in school, but she will never forget her capacity to think analytically, critically, and creatively."

For Dr. Adams, a lecture was a loving event. The act of love is essentially an act of giving something significant from ourselves—attention, knowledge, support, a smile, touch, care, warmth, or beauty. To be genuine, this kind of act should originate from the mind, heart, and will of the person who performs the act. It is a human act at its best. Isn't the artist who seeks to create beauty a lover? Isn't the scientist who advances human knowledge, the novelist who writes an insightful novel, or the social reformer who strives to create the condition of a better society a lover? Isn't the person who helps her fellow citizens in time of need a lover? Similarly, isn't the teacher who provokes the student to think and grow as a human individual a lover? A lecturer who merely transmits ideas or in some way conveys ideas to the student is a messenger, not a lover. How can you influence your students constructively, productively if what you communicate in your lecture does not originate from your heart, mind, and will? The mere transmission of ideas may help the student become a good business, engineering, car, or computer technician, but how about the growth of the student as a human individual? Generally speaking, students are ignorant, in the sense that they do not possess certain types of knowledge and experiences when they come to school—this is why they come school—but they are not stupid. On the contrary, they are very intelligent. They can easily distinguish between the genuine teacher and the messenger.

This meditation, which was more a reverie than a reflective train of thought, was interrupted by the sound of approaching footsteps of two nurses, one pushing a bed and the other holding an IV apparatus connected to Dr. Adams's left arm. Dr. Lawson left his chair and stood in the corner of the room the moment the nurses moved in. Janice, who was in charge of the IV apparatus, greeted Dr. Lawson with a friendly but sad "good morning" and then helped the other nurses move Dr. Adams's fragile body to his bed. He was unconscious. "He had acute, awful chest pains last night," she told Dr. Lawson as she was adjusting her patient's pillows. "His blood pressure was out of control for a while. We almost lost him were it not for the caring eyes of his attending nurse. Dr. Jenkins took X-rays of both lungs. He thinks that the left lung is degenerating faster than the right one, which is not good news! But he will recover his consciousness rather soon and his strength a little later. Dr. Jenkins prescribed a stronger painkiller."

Dr. Lawson moved closer to Janice and hugged her. He tried to speak, but he could not. The words were so heavily loaded with emotions, they could not move through his lips. He pressed her shoulder tenderly and nodded softly as he was freeing her from his hug. Their eyes met. They spoke a kind of language only the human heart could understand. He moved slowly to the side of the bed and gazed into his friend's sleeping eyes for a few, but long, seconds and said, "Janice, I shall be back as soon as I deliver my afternoon lecture. He left the room slowly, pensively.

Dr. Daniel Harris, member of the history department, was sitting next to Dr. Adams's bed when Dr. Lawson later arrived at the scene. He was concerned about Dr. Adams's health, but he did not know about the devastating crisis that had befallen him the night before. "Bring a chair. We shall need you."

Before he joined his colleague, Dr. Lawson moved toward his friend's bed and greeted him with a smile. He held his hand and pressed it affectionately. Dr. Adams felt its warmth. Dr. Lawson moved his left hand and allowed it to join his right hand in holding Dr. Adams's frail hand as warmly as he could. "How do you feel?" Dr. Lawson asked.

"How do I feel? Now I feel better, much better," he said with a soft smile.

"We would appreciate it immensely, Daniel, if you could join us in a conversation we are having about the ideals of Webster as a liberal arts institution. Pull your chair closer," Dr. Lawson said. "I heard that the dean has formed committee to revise the mission statement of the college," Dr. Lawson remarked. "He thinks that it will be useful in our next fundraising campaign—did I hear you correctly?" Stanley asked, looking at Dr. Harris.

"You did."

"How is it going?"

"A little rocky, and frankly a little messy," Dr. Lawson remarked. "I have a feeling that some members of the committee, and I am one of them, are not clear about the essential elements of liberal arts education: What makes a human being a liberally educated person? What are the building blocks, or ingredients, that constitute the structure and identity of this kind of educated person? What kind of human character should we prepare for society? I thought that the mission statement of a college should convey to the public the kind of values the college stands for and the kind of character it cultivates.

"It seems to me that philosophers and social scientists should be in charge of drafting this kind of document. This proposal is based on two assumptions: first, the study of values and ideals is the specialty of philosophers, and second, the study of human character is the specialty of both philosophers and social scientists. The philosopher should provide a conception of the ideals the college should uphold, and the scientist should, in cooperation with the philosopher, provide an adequate analysis of the conditions under which these ideals can be implemented. They should also cooperate on articulating a reasonable conception of the structure of human character. If this is the case, and I think it is, the first step in composing a mission statement is to define the ideals of the college."

"But," Dr. Harris intervened, "can the philosopher compose such a statement without assuming a certain view of human character, at least the character we aim to cultivate as a college?"

"You are right," Dr. Lawson admitted. "A conception of the ideals of the college presupposes a view of the kind of human character we aim to cultivate, and contrariwise, a view of such character presupposes a conception of the ideals of the college. But the proposal I have made is based on the assumption, which many see as biased, viz., that the philosopher possesses adequate knowledge of the basic elements of human character—"

"We seem to be caught in some kind of circular reasoning," Dr. Harris intervened. "Is there a way out of this circle?"

Dr. Harris could not continue the discussion because Janice entered the room with a pitcher of water and two empty glasses. She stopped in the middle of the room before moving to Dr. Adams's side of the bed and greeted these two academicians with a mysterious smile. She instinctively approved this unusual spectacle. Whatever pleased her patient also pleased her heart. "I do not wish to interrupt your conversation," she said. "I just need to check on my patient." She cast a quick look at Dr. Adams's bed. It was fine. "Do you need anything, Dr. Adams?" she wondered.

"No, my dear, not now. Thank you!"

"I shall be back shortly," she said and left.

"Frankly," Dr. Harris said after Janice left, "I came here for two reasons. First, I desire to check on my dear and honored colleague, Seneca. I and many members of the faculty miss him. He has been on my mind and the minds of the humanities division, especially those in the Humanities Center. 'It seems that when the door of Seneca's office is closed,' Dr. Stephenson said to me the other day, 'that the whole center is closed. The corridor of the building is dim, lifeless, without the light of his presence.'"

It was clear to Dr. Lawson that Daniel was ignorant of the actual condition of Dr. Adams's situation. A warm look from Dr. Lawson's eyes traveled slowly to Dr. Adams's eyes. Dr. Adams nodded but remained silent. It may strike the reader as strange that not only Dr. Davis but the whole faculty was ignorant of the fact that Dr. Adams had been dying slowly for the last few months and that he had been performing his part-time teaching and administrative duties stoically until the past few weeks without disclosing the nature of his sickness to anyone except to his friend Dr. Lawson, to his family, and to the dean. He had decided to be productive until the store of his energy was depleted. The dean was willing to replace him temporarily only because he could not believe that the celebrated philosopher of Webster College would leave the world! Dr. Adams was the strongest pillar of the college.

"Second," Dr. Davis continued, "I need to know his view of the ideals Webster College advocates as a liberal arts institution. No one in this college is more qualified to answer this question adequately than this wise, honorable human being."

Dr. Adams shook his head softly when he heard those words. He stretched his hand to the pitcher that Janice had brought, but Dr. Lawson preceded him. He poured water into one of the two glasses and handed it to his friend. Dr. Adams took a sip and smiled.

"I am not sure that Harris's remark about me is accurate. I am neither wise nor honorable, although I have always striven to possess these two virtues."

"What I said," Dr. Harris responded, "represents the view of every teacher and student who had any meaningful encounter with you, Seneca. You are our philosopher, and you are our teacher. I only hope that you can shed some light on the kind of mission statement we should draft. No one knows better than you the history, the problems, the strengths and weaknesses, the potentialities, and the possible conditions under which the college can become a better institution of higher learning."

Dr. Adams took another sip of water and fixed a timid look at Dr. Harris. "I may try to express my opinion, no more, with the understanding that an opinion is not verified knowledge and that it can be wrong."

"This is all I need—your opinion. The committee will be infinitely grateful to you for any ray of light you may care to shed on this question."

"I am weak, as you can see, so I entreat you to be patient with me."

"You can take all the time you need. I shall keep listening to you now and in the next days until I hear the last word from you on this subject."

"You give me more credit than I deserve, Daniel."

"I wish I could give you the credit you truly deserve."

Dr. Adams sank into a reflective mood for a few moments and then said, "An inquiry into the nature of ideals, regardless of whether they are religious, moral, political, artistic, philosophical, scientific, or cultural, should begin with an understanding of human nature—the features, capacities, or elements that make us human. We are physical, or biological, beings like the rest of natural objects, but we are *also human beings*. What is the nature of this human dimension? I raise this question because an ideal is something people value and pursue as an essential need, as something indispensable for their existence as human beings or for the achievement of their happiness. There are two types of human needs, biological and human. I here assume that the physical dimension is an integral part of the biological dimension. Although biological needs are human and essential for our being, I shall focus my attention on the needs that are distinctively human. We may view biological needs as necessary conditions for the realization of the distinctively human needs: what do we need, or desire, as human beings?

"Broadly speaking, ideals are practical responses to human needs. They are, moreover, human constructs, for example, truth, beauty, or freedom. They function as guideposts, and I would say guidelights, that illuminate the method and conditions under which we meet our human needs. Again, they function as standards in the evaluation of the different types of decisions we make in the course of our ordinary or practical lives. Next, every ideal embodies or expresses a basic human value of something dear to us as human beings, as something we prize not only because it is a means to the fulfillment of a certain need but also because we view it as an intrinsic good, as something valuable in itself. For example, we need knowledge, but we also treat knowledge as intrinsically valuable. Don't we delight in the act of knowing, that is, of discovering knowledge about a natural or human object? Don't we sometimes have an Archimedes eureka experience regardless of the type of object we know or discover?

"A need signifies a lack: we need what we lack, or what we do not have. This is an important reason why we place value on the object we need. We need shelter, food, and water, and we need knowledge, love, and freedom. This is why we place value on any object in any one of these categories of need. These and similar needs inhere in us as 'strivings' in our physical constitution as human beings. Their unity constitutes what I would call 'human nature.' This nature exists in us as a potentiality primarily because the strivings that signify the needs exist as potentialities in the physical constitution of the human being. For example, I desire beauty and love because I do not have them and because there is a striving in me to have them. I feel thirst for water, and I feel hunger for food when I am hungry or thirsty. I here assume that desire is a striving, a kind of propulsive power or drive. It is an intentional or purposeful drive or thrust toward an object or a kind of object. It derives its propulsive power from the nagging itch of a need. The desire for knowledge derives from the need to know. This desire exists as a potentiality in the fabric of human nature just as the desire for food exists in the physical constitution of the human being as a potentiality. This claim necessarily implies that human strivings—that is, striving for truth, beauty, goodness, or freedom—exist as potentialities in our biological constitution. I was not born with knowledge but with the potentiality to know;

I was not born with a good heart but with the potentiality to develop one; I was not born with a sense of aesthetic beauty but with the potentiality to acquire one; and I was not born as a free person but with the potentiality to become free. Any examination of human nature is in effect an examination of these and similar potentialities. The desire for food or drink exists in us as ready-made strivings, unlike human potentialities. The child seeks food the moment it is born, if not before, but it does not seek knowledge until it grows and matures rationally.

"There are two types of needs: natural and artificial. The first are given, and they inhere in the fabric of our biological and human constitution. The second are individual or social; they originate from reflection, conditioning, or allurements. I was born with the need for food but not with the need for reading mystery novels or driving fancy cars. The first are natural, and the second are acquired. The first are essential to our growth and development as human beings; the second may or may not be essential to our human growth and development. The emphasis in this conversation is on the essential needs, on those that promote our human well-being. What are these needs?

"We may distinguish four essential human needs, each one of which is the basis of a central human value. The first is cognitive in nature and aims at the value of truth; the second is artistic in nature and aims at the value of beauty; the third is practical in nature and aims at the value of goodness; and the fourth is personal in nature and aims at the value of freedom. Meeting these needs is the basis of personal perfection or well-being. The ideal that underlies this need originates from one's vision or understanding of herself as a particular, unique individual. This ideal does not originate from one reflective act but evolves gradually as we grow in the early period of our life.

"These four values are ideals and as such are general in character. Each one embraces a set of particular values. Truth embraces values such as wisdom, erudition, and sound judgment; goodness embraces values such as justice, friendship, and honesty; beauty embraces values such as elegance, sublimity, and tragedy; and freedom embraces values sch as pleasure, success, and longevity.

"We desire truth, goodness, beauty, and freedom because they are essential needs. Growth in the attainment or realization of these needs is tantamount to growth in our humanity: the more we grow in their realization, the more human we become, the more fulfilled we become. I tend to think that human growth and development is the ultimate source of human happiness. Don't we feel profoundly satisfied when we grow in our knowledge of nature, the history of human civilization, the biology and psychology of human beings, the nature of art, the nature of evil, or the dynamics of the cosmic process? Don't we derive deep satisfaction from reading literary works or contemplating important paintings, listening to serious music, or watching a tragedy unfold before our eyes on the stage? Don't we feel truly satisfied when we love and receive love, when we help our neighbor, or when we share moments of pleasure or sadness with a dear friend? Don't we feel a sense of well-being, of pride, when we succeed in our professional life or when we recognize that our children are good and successful citizens?" Dr. Adams paused for a moment, drank some water, and then threw a friendly smile at Dr. Harris. "Yes, human ideals function as the basis of a worthwhile life. They are the most reliable standards in our evaluation of the true, the good, the beautiful, and human perfection, and they are such standards because they express the most refined intuition of the essential strivings of human nature, of the sense of importance in our lives. I here assume that the human spark from which these strivings arise is intrinsically valuable, therefore sacred. No authority on the face of the earth can justify or violate its integrity—"

Dr. Adams suddenly stopped. He drank some more water. "I think I need a short break, Stanley."

But Stanley, who knew quite well his friend's condition, left the room and rushed to the nurses' station. He returned with Janice and a paper cup that contained painkillers. Janice moved gently to the side of Dr. Adams's bed, poured some water into an empty cup, and gave the medication to her patient. Although he was experiencing intense pain, he smiled when his eyes met Janice's eyes. "Why don't you rest for a moment?" Janice said.

"This pain is a nuisance, Janice," he softly murmured when she placed a pain tablet in his hand. But the nurse, who understood the good professor, remained silent. She only clutched her teeth behind firmly pursed lips. She was unable to respond to him. The only word that slipped from her lips was "Please!" Dr. Adams could not stop the surge of a mysterious chuckle from the depth of his being when he heard that "please."

"I believe in the existence of God because there are angels in this world. I am blessed with this angel!" He held Janice's hand and kissed it. "You are a divine presence!" he said in a faint voice.

An expression of confusion, one permeated with surprise, emanated from Dr. Adams's face. He was not expecting this kind of scene. He simply looked at Dr. Lawson with inquiring eyes.

"Seneca is being visited by an unexpected bout of severe pain. He will—"

"Oh, my goodness!" Dr. Harris, frightened, said, interrupting his colleague. "I am terribly sorry. I must have burdened you with my questions, Seneca! Please forgive me!"

"There is nothing to forgive!" Dr. Adams said. "Pain has been my friend for a long time, Daniel. I miss him when he does not visit me regularly."

"Oh no!" Dr. Davis retorted. But Dr. Adams did not accept his retort. "You need to rest. I should leave. I can return at a more opportune time," Dr. Harris murmured, "only to see you."

"You cannot leave until we finish our conversation," Dr. Adams said.

"Wait a little!" Dr. Lawson interjected, addressing Dr. Harris. "Let him rest for a minute or two. He will feel better if he answers your questions sufficiently." Dr. Adams nodded approvingly.

And, in fact, the painkiller Dr. Adams had taken was strong, effective. He was able to regain command of his ideas within a few minutes, during which the two colleagues chatted about the latest news of the college.

"Daniel," Dr. Adams said when the right moment arrived, "you are a historian. Please take a short respite from the stream of social life; sit on a hill adjacent to the flow of this stream and observe it as a social scientist. Focus your attention on what human beings do and what they have been doing as individuals and societies from the dawn of history until the present. Let us now ask, What is the substance of their activities? Again, what is human history about? If I were to answer this question in one word, I can say that humans struggle, and have been struggling, to live. This is what they did in the past, and this is what they shall be doing in the future. Living is their destiny! They go to school; they work; they get married; they seek pleasure; they build societies, institutions, and organizations; they grow old; and then they die. At the communal level, they create laws and governments to manage their lives. Moreover, they create a human world based on their knowledge of themselves and the nature of the world. But although people nowadays live in this kind of world; although their ways of living are different from the ways people lived in the past; although they are more, or less, advanced scientifically, artistically, philosophically, and technologically; their supreme aim is one and the same: to live! Would you agree to this very sketchy answer to my question?"

"No one can disagree with you, Seneca!"

"Good. Now let me ask you, why do people do their best to build this marvelous world of civilization, and why, in their capacities as scientists, artists, philosophers, social reformers, teachers, engineers, farmers, and religious leaders, do they participate in the ritual of building this world?"

"To live, to live well, to live better, always better."

"Fine! In fact," Dr. Harris added, "we see this tendency—and some would characterize it as an overpowering tendency in human nature—in individuals, communities, and nations, and we see it in the different areas of human endeavor. It is a kind of driving force. Let me emphasize that it is not merely a drive to live but to *live better, always better*."

"But," Dr. Adams intervened, "how do you explain the fact that a large number of people, maybe most of them, are satisfied merely with living? All they want is shelter, enough food, security, clothes, some leisure, and a few morsels of pleasure. Those who strive to be artists, philosophers, scientists, lawmakers, or inventors—in short, creators and leaders in the different spheres of human life—are few, very few."

"I agree that this is the status quo, and it seems that it has always been the case. But the point in question is not how people actually live now or how they lived in the past, but how they *can live always better*. Why or how they actually live is a practical question, a question of education and social or scientific engineering. Can we provide an explanation of the phenomenon of progress in all the domains of human life without the actuality or possibility of this essential striving? Can we explain the impulse of creativity in art, science, philosophy, technology, social reform without assuming this striving? Now let us pay a visit to a person who seems content with 'just living.' Let us show this person two movies, vividly depicting his present life, the life with which he is contented, and the other movie depicting him leading a better life, one he would dream of in idle moments or when he reads idealistic novels. Let us have a conversation with this human being. 'If we give you a choice between the life you are leading now and the better life, which would you prefer?' He would certainly prefer the second choice, and he would add that if he thought that this choice was possible, he would do all he could to live the better way of life. Now, do you think, David, that this hypothetical conversation is both realistic and reasonable? Do you also think that most if not all people would recognize the difference among living, living well, and living better? Do you moreover think that they would choose to live the better way of life if it is possible?"

"Yes."

"The purpose of expressing my point this way is to emphasize that, regardless of the way of life people are actually leading, the desire to live a better way of life is an essential striving that exists as a potentiality in human nature."

"But what does it mean to lead a 'better' way of life? What kind of life constitutes 'good' living?" Dr. Harris asked.

"A good life consists of meeting the essential needs of human nature, which we have already discussed, viz., the need to know, to appreciate beauty, to be moral, and to realize oneself as a human individual. The activity of living well is substantially an activity meeting these needs."

"Excellent!! It should, then, follow that this kind of life is human par excellence—yes, but under what conditions can these needs be met?" Dr. Harris asked.

"Two basic conditions should be met in order to meet them. First, they should be based on the values, or ideals, that arise as a response to these very needs: truth, beauty, goodness, and creation. These values function as standards for the kinds of decisions in our endeavor to meet those needs. Practically, all the situations that occasion these needs in the process of daily living involve one or a combination of these values. This claim is based on the assumption that these needs arise from essential demands of human nature. For example, we need to survive physically, but the question is how. Can we steal, lie, deceive, or cheat when we meet these needs? People secure their survival in different ways. Some ways are better, more correct, more prudently conceived than others. What is the best possible way we can choose to meet this need? But we encounter the same question in the different spheres of our lives—family, workplace, school, art, religious institution, friendship, personal life, and the different social encounters in the different circumstances of our lives. We constantly face the question, how should we act in our attempt to meet this or that particular need? Broadly, the way we meet them should be rational, and to be rational, it should satisfy a basic striving of human nature according to the demands of the value relevant to that situation. We should always remember that meeting a need is a personal responsibility. Duty and punishment are not transferable.

"Second, regardless of the extent of its accuracy, folly, rationality, or wisdom of the way we meet it, a need should originate from our minds, hearts, and wills. This condition is based on the assumption that no one can live our lives; consequently, no one can assume responsibility, credit, or blame for the actions we choose; therefore, no one can decide how we should live except us as individuals. Don't we revolt when someone, even if she happens to be a parent or a friend, tells us what to do or how we should live? Who knows how the individual feels, thinks, desires, or dreams better, or more, than the individual herself or himself? Besides, how can we feel inner or genuine satisfaction if we act or live according to the will of another person or power? How can we assume responsibility for our actions if the action does not originate from our mind, heart, and will?

"We grow and become the individuals we are in the process of meeting our human needs. If in living a good life we respond to the essential needs of human nature, if these needs exist in us as potentialities, if they come to life in the process of living, then it should follow that the way we meet them will necessarily determine the kind of individual we are and the kind of life we lead; it should also follow that the values we live will be translated into dispositions, inclinations, and habits. For example, acting according to the value of courage will generate a disposition or inclination to act courageously in future situations that require courageous acts. The unity of the different dispositions, inclinations, and habits in the individual constitutes what philosophers and psychologists have called 'human character.' Thus, human character is the unity of the way a person acts morally, aesthetically, intellectually, creatively, socially, religiously, individually, politically, and materially. Any dimension of character is the source and basis of the different types of action we perform in the course of our daily life. Accordingly, the actions we perform, or the life we lead, always *reflects* the kind of character we are. How else can we say that 'by their actions you shall know them'?

"But the structure of the human character exists in us as a bundle of potentialities and not as ready-made realities. As potentialities, they are a possibility for boundless realization. Is there a limit to how much we can love; know; appreciate beautiful objects; and create new ways of thinking, feeling, and acting; or how much we can expand the horizon of every dimension of our individual being? No. This is why it is, I think, reasonable to say that the life of the individual is a continual process of growth and development.

"Now, if the supreme aim of human life is living well, always better; if this kind of life originates from one's mind, heart, and will; if it consists of realizing the essential strivings in human nature; again, if these strivings exist as potentialities in need of realization, then I can propose that the *supreme aim of liberal education is, or should be, the cultivation of human character.*"

"But," Dr. Harris intervened, "how does this definition of the aim of liberal education relate to or in any way shed light on the mission statement our committee is trying to draft, especially on the kinds of ideals the college should pursue?"

"First, any ideals we envision should either emanate from or be founded in the supreme aim of the college. We should treat them as guideposts or as a basis for translating the meaning of the aim into concrete, definable measures or steps, that is, into particular experiences that promote the continual realization of this aim. Put differently, the ideals should be viewed as the arms and legs of the aim. Thus, if the aim of the college is the cultivation of the character of the student, if this cultivation consists of realizing the fundamental potentialities of the student, it should follow that the task of the college is to create the conditions for realizing these potentialities. How? Let me answer this question, which may strike some as rhetorical, by an example.

"Direct your attention at the cognitive faculty as a striving of human nature. Here the task of the college should be to nurture the mind of the student in two ways. First, it should cultivate it in the arts of observation, conceptual analysis, perspicacity, logical or critical thinking, and making sound judgment. Every course offered in the different academic departments, especially in the humanities, should foster the art of critical thinking and making sound judgment. I emphasize this art because it is an essential condition of success in academic inquiry and practical life. Who can underestimate the value of sound judgment in the sphere of family, school, work, social life, personal life, and the different institutions of society? The point is to train the mind of the student to think from within. Second, the task of the college is to introduce the mind of the student to the various types of knowledge in the different sciences and humanities. The purpose of acquiring this knowledge is not to stuff the mind with stale ideas but with living and relevant ideas. Even the most difficult ideas of physics, biology, metaphysics, anthropology, and chemistry can be translated by a competent teacher into living, meaningful ideas. No idea of an aspect of human or natural reality is irrelevant to the mind of the student. Living ideas are powers. They illuminate and empower the mind in its effort to understand the complexity of the different situations of theoretical and practical life. Francis Bacon was not mistaken when he said that knowledge is power. But it is power only when it is an integral element of the cognitive faculty, that is, when the mind sees, feels, and thinks in terms of the knowledge it acquires. How many a student keeps the ideas she receives from the teacher as a trust without comprehending their meaning or implications for her life and then returns the same ideas to the teacher at the final examination only to receiver a high or passing grade? Unfortunately, in most of the courses taught our college, learning, and consequently knowing, consists of memorizing ideas passively. I have seen with my own eyes, when I was a student and later when I became a teacher, how so many students fold the notes they wrote during the semester and throw them in the wastebasket of the classroom soon after the semester ends. This practice does reflect good or real teaching and learning. Every course taught at Webster should be an occasion for growth in the art of critical thinking and making sound judgment. How many a friendship or marriage fails because of bad judgment? How many a life or business venture becomes a misadventure? How many an employee loses her job? In short, how many a plan has faltered because of unsound judgment? I do not exaggerate if I say that the most important gift a liberal arts institution offers to its students is proficiency in making sound judgment in personal and public life. This proficiency is a necessary condition for successful living.

"I tend to think, Daniel, that a statement of mission of the college should revolve around two main ideas: the aim and the ideals of the college as a liberal arts institution. We have discussed both ideas. First, the aim of the college should be the cultivation of human character. This claim is based on the assumption that the purpose of human life is living well, always better, and that a cultivated character acts from a sense of value, that it is proficient in the art of making sound judgment and committed to the good life. Second, the ideals of the college are the values of truth, beauty, goodness, and creation. The structure of the curriculum should be based on the unity of these values. We can view them as responses to essential needs of human nature. Their realization in our life is what makes it worth living.

"The proposal that the mission statement should revolve around these two ideals assumes that education is a lifelong process. It may begin at a liberal arts institution or at an earlier level, but it should not end at graduation day because growth in our humanity is a lifelong process. The more we grow and develop as human beings, the more fulfilled we become, the more we can grow and develop as human individuals. This assertion is based on the assumption, which we have already discussed, that the human dimension of our being is the possibility for boundless realization. This is the secret, and this is the glory, of human nature. The task of the liberal arts institution is to equip the student with the knowledge and skill required for the possibility of this kind of education. Some time ago, Socrates argued that genuine learning is self-learning. We should heed this gem of wisdom. I always viewed Webster College as an institution that aims to teach its students how to teach themselves, not to indoctrinate them in a certain ideology."

"Let me confess to you, Seneca, that I am even skeptical about the wisdom or utility of revising the mission statement of the college."

"Why?" Dr. Adams asked, interrupting his colleague.

"Because I wonder whether it is practicable. Do we apply the present mission statement adequately?"

"What do you mean?"

"Suppose we write a highly informed, idealistic statement, and suppose the dean and the president use it effectively in attracting the money of generous donors, which is doubtful? Is the college willing to restructure the curriculum according to its demands or requirements? Or is it, as I have just indicated, simply a decorative emblem? By the way, who reads such a statement? Most if not all the faculty, not to mention the recently hired ones, teach courses, and the courses they teach are assigned to them. They do not really view themselves as agents or representatives of liberal arts education, much less as embodiments of the spirit of this kind of education. Do they focus their attention when they teach on the ideals contained in the mission statement? Have they even read it? This is a big issue, I know, but I raise the question only because I wonder whether the mission of the college is also the mission of the faculty member who struggles to live. Perhaps we should discuss this question in a special conversation."

"Yes, we should," Dr. Adams said and fell into a reflective stance for a moment. "Ideals," he said when he regained his normal consciousness, "are divine stars. They hang as divine stars in the sky of the human world. They are the object of reflection in our attempt to understand the mystery of nature, of existence, and the difficult questions and problems of human life at the individual and communal levels. They—"

Dr. Adams could not complete his response to Dr. Harris because a lady pushing a rack of food trays stopped at the door of the room. "Dinner-time!" she announced as she moved a tray from the rack and then placed it at the side table that sat next to Dr. Adams's bed. "Bon appétit!" she said and retreated to her rack.

"My goodness! I have overstayed my visit," Dr. Harris blurted out as he was preparing himself to leave. "I have burdened you beyond the call of courtesy." Embarrassed, he added in a somewhat hasty manner, "I am pro-foundly grateful to you, Seneca. I wish the other members of the committee could listen to your analysis of the ideals of the college. But I shall convey your ideas to them. What you said is exactly what we need in drafting the mission statement of the college. I cannot thank you enough, Seneca!" Then he turned his attention to Dr. Lawson. "I shall see you soon, Stanley!"

"Not at all!" Dr. Adams said. "I am thankful to you for luring me into this meaningful conversation." He paused for a second and then added, "We did not finish it. You should come back soon—I hope. This topic, Dan-iel, is dear to my heart. I wish I were a member of your committee!"

Dr. Harris shook Dr. Lawson's hand warmly and bid him goodbye. On his way out of the room, he looked back and said, "But I promise to return only to see how you are progressing!"

Janice, who had peeked through the door twice during that conversa-tion mainly to see whether she was needed, entered the room with a cheer-ful "Good day!" She was happy to see her patient in a lively mood. She seriously believed that people who could thrive as human beings during the last days of their lives deserved the utmost respect, love, and care. She saw in them human refinement, true human beauty. *It is a pleasure to be in the presence of such people*, she thought. She viewed them as jewels of inspiration, of human light. She treated them with a feeling of awe. There is a big difference between standing in the presence of human mediocrity and human excellence. By its very essence, human excellence is charming, lovable. Janice was delighting in this kind of feeling when Dr. Harris left. Her immediate desire was to feed her patient, but Dr. Lawson had already stolen this privilege from her. He was adjusting the side table to his friend's convenience.

"How is my patient doing?" she asked tenderly. Dr. Adams stretched his hand to her. She clasped it. Dr. Adams bent his body a little and kissed her hand. This kiss, which she had received on more than one occasion during the past few days, was a precious gift to her because it was delivered by a loving heart. We frequently feel the depth of a true human heart more by a kiss, a touch, or a look than by ornate speeches, material gifts, or delicious pastries. The pleasure of the mind and heart is superior to any pleasure we receive from material objects and social encounters. Although the people who are capable of giving and receiving it are rare, we sometimes meet them in strange circumstances and ways. Genuine humanity does not hide itself; it glitters with its warmth, with its light. The fact that baffles the rational mind is that the majority of human eyes cannot see this kind of glitter. It takes time, wisdom, and caring to cultivate *human eyes*. But alas! Can one have such eyes if one does not possess a true human heart?

"I am fine, my dear!" Dr. Adams said.

"You are in good hands," she said. "I shall return with your medications after you eat your supper. I feel at ease when Dr. Lawson is around you."

Dr. Lawson smiled without uttering word. Indeed, Dr. Lawson was a true friend, the kind Cicero and Seneca the stoic philosophers sang about in their writings. He was a professor of physics. When he had first arrived at Webster, Dr. Lawson discovered that Dr. Adams was deeply interested in cosmology. Dr. Lawson had read the works of Plato, Spinoza, Hegel, and Whitehead, but he was desirous to explore the thought of the most recent cosmologists such as Hawkins. When Dr. Adams offered a seminar in the philosophy of Whitehead, whose cosmology was founded in contemporary physics, Dr. Lawson felt an irresistible desire to enroll in that seminar, and he did. By the end of the semester, the two men discovered each other not only as thinkers but also as human beings. This discovery was the starting point of a true friendship, which grew in depth as the months and years marched into the future.

Dr. Lawson was married and had two children, a son, Kenny, and a daughter, Eve. His wife, Jasmine, was a history teacher at Murrah High School. She and her husband treated Dr. Adams as a member of their family. Sunday was not a Sunday for them if Dr. Adams did not join them for lunch. The children loved him so much, they called him Uncle Seneca. Eve, who had just graduated from high school, lamented the fact that she would not be able to study philosophy with Uncle Seneca. In a way, and next to their parents, Eve and Kenny always sought his counsel and support when they faced personal problems or needed help on a certain academic question. Dr. Adams was a luminous presence in their lives, and they were a blessing in his life.

Dr. Lawson was standing next to his friend's bed not simply to watch him eat his meal but also to make sure that he *was* eating it. The fact that the remainder of Dr. Adams's life was short did not matter. To Dr. Lawson, every living day with his friend was a lifetime, one he could not squander.

At that very moment, Eve walked into the room almost on tiptoe, with two eyes fixed on Dr. Adams's face. He was trying to masticate a piece of salmon when she moved closer to his bed. She greeted him with "Uncle Seneca!" But Uncle Seneca's eyes had already embraced her with a welcoming, compassionate look. She kissed him on the right cheek and then moved to the other side of the bed and kissed her father, also on the right cheek. "How do you feel, Uncle Seneca?" Eve asked with a tender voice. "We miss you very much!"

"I too miss you, dear Eve! How is your mother?"

"She is doing well. She plans to visit you very soon. She has been grading some papers. She has baked your favorite pie," Eve said. She opened her handbag and pulled out a package containing a big slice of apple pie. "She wants you to eat it with your supper tonight."

"You arrived at the right time, my dear. Thank you! Convey my gratitude to your mother, please. Did you eat your supper?"

"No, we have been waiting for my father. My mother cannot eat without my father."

"I understand," Dr. Adams said with a nod and a smile on his lips. Then he looked at his friend and graced his face with another smile.

"Tell your mother that I shall be at home in a few minutes, Eve. I shall leave Uncle Seneca as soon as he finishes his meal," Dr. Lawson said, interrupting Dr. Adams.

"I shall, Dad, but I would like to tell Uncle Seneca something confidential before I leave."

"Do you want me to leave the room?" her father asked.

"No, I shall whisper it to him.

"We love you so much, Uncle. We have lit a candle of love for you. My mother placed it at the windowsill of the kitchen. It will remain shining until you visit us again. We are praying for you!" she said and kissed him again on his cheek. He tried to speak but could not because tears gathered in his eyes. Eve vanished in less than a second when she glimpsed those tears.

"I cannot eat!" Dr. Adams said after Eve left. "I feel satisfied, full to the brim, Stanley!"

"But please try," Dr. Lawson said. He did not press his friend to eat because he saw the tears and because he saw how his daughter had left—as if she were being swept out of the room by an imperceptible force. "Would you eat the pie?"

"I shall eat it a little later."

"Promise?"

"Yes. Your family is waiting for you. Please, go!" Dr. Adams said.

"I shall be back later this evening."

"I look with anticipation to seeing you then"

And the two friends met later that evening. Dr. Adams was eating his pie when Dr. Lawson arrived at the scene. Susan, the attending nurse that evening, was watching him eat it. Dr. Lawson did not directly greet his friend. He simply stood at the door and watched his friend enjoy his dessert. When she saw him gazing at his friend, the nurse said, "I shall leave for a few minutes. Dr. Hardy prescribed new medications for you, one for pain and the other for breathing. He will see you when he makes the evening rounds."

Dr. Lawson moved the side table away from Dr. Adams's bed and sat next to him.

"You constantly worry about me," said Dr. Adams, "and your eyes are constantly watching me. I feel that your presence in my life is firmer than the orbits of the earth around the sun. I do not need the arguments of the philosophers, miracles, or the magical wand of the church to believe in the existence of the divine. You are the finest rays of this presence in my life. No human being can wish, or even dream, of a finer presence! I cannot express to you any feelings of gratitude, for such feelings stand as ridiculous, lame, drole witnesses at the door of my heart, nor do I need to express the sense of happiness that brightens my mind from the fact that I am a beneficiary of your luminous presence, for neither poetic nor philosophical means of expression can embody the depth of my happiness."

Dr. Adams paused for a few seconds, took in a deep breath, and made an attempt to resume his conversation, but Dr. Lawson intervened. "What you have just said was not said by you but by the divine spark in you. I see it and I feel it. Please, try to rest a little, at least just before Dr. Hardy arrives."

"I shall comply with your request. But then you will have to shoulder the task of speaking. How was your afternoon lecture?"

"My lecture was good, but not the state of the college—"

"State of the college?" Dr. Adams exclaimed, interrupting Dr. Lawson.

"Yes, the college!"

"Tell me, what happened? What is going on??"

"The lid on a quiet scandal was removed this morning. The president has been having an affair with his secretary for more than a year. They eloped two days ago. His wife and children are agitated, beside themselves, and the board of trustees are frantic. They held two urgent meetings, one yesterday and the second today. They have decided to ask Dean Beardsley to be the acting president and Dr. Robin Knight to be the acting dean. The chairman of the board argued that a college cannot function without a president, not for one day, because a college without a president is like a human being without a head. The president is the mind of the college. We can live without a dean for a year or two, but we cannot live without a president for that long because the president embodies the unity of the college. Without him, the sense of responsibility on campus would collapse."

"Never mind this poor argument, but Beardsley?" Dr. Adams wondered loudly.

Dr. Lawson shook his head with an expression of concern on his face. "This is the real problem. Presidents, deans, and students come and go, but the faculty stay. Some of them become fixtures! The real question is whether Landy will represent the interests of the students and the faculty. He could hardly function as a dean. I heard that many of the instructors are very disappointed. How can the president of the board emphasize the role of the president if the board chooses incompetent leaders? I heard that the academic committee of the board opposed the chairman's decision, but as usual, he silenced all objections directly or indirectly."

"It seems to me," Dr. Adams intervened, "that the college needs a strong dean. She or he is supposed to be the patron of the faculty and the guardian of the curriculum and the teaching process. Her character and vision of liberal arts education should be the impetus of the growth and development of the college. But choosing King is worrisome, if not disastrous—why him? You know what Mcleod thinks; you also know his view of the religion department. This department is in shambles. He thinks that Beardsley is the most inefficient department chair in the college."

"Beardsley is his man."

"And the dean?"

"This means that in his capacity as acting president, he will indirectly steer the direction, even decisions, of the search committee in the name of consultation, advice, and general guidance."

"I tend to think that Beardsley will be appointed as official dean of the college sooner than we think."

"If what you say happens, Stanley, I am almost certain that the college will be marching on a downward path. Wise, visionary, and loyal leadership is the key to the progress of any institution, academic or otherwise. The faculty may propose ideas and programs, and they may design the most idealistic and realistic curriculum and most innovative projects, but those proposals will remain ink on paper if they are not implemented. Scholars speak of political, religious, and social will, but we should also speak of academic will. The dean should be the concrete embodiment of this will. Beardsley is not his own man, and he is will-less! He was the man of the dean, and he will be the man of the new president or acting president. He is not even his own man. He will be the man of the president in matters of general policy and of his cronies in matters of the daily activities and projects of the college. He is a yes man, and the yes is always to the ears that keep him in his office. Political philosophers call it 'survival.'"

"But how do such leaders function? How do they perform their duties?"

"The question is whether they function! This is a rhetorical response, I know, but you will be surprised to know that many of those who sit in the highest chair of an institution do not actually function. The established institution runs its course thanks to the previous leaders and in some cases founders. But the question that should merit our attention is, Can the board appoint an acting president, even acting dean, without the consent and effective advice of the faculty, at least the academic council?

"In fact, and behind the scenes, the opinion or advice of the faculty is always secondary. You should always wonder, Who is the faculty? Most of the time they hear about this or that decision or about this or that policy. Even in faculty meetings, how many faculty members speak, express their opinion, determine policy, or make decisions? Faculty apathy is a silent cancer in many colleges and universities! There is a big difference between form and content. Formally, the faculty counts, but existentially? In certain cases, what the president says is final, and in others, what the dean says is final.

"Dean Beardsley is a shining example of hypocrisy. He is a slick speaker—smooth and seemingly logical, but in fact he is not a dean; it is more appropriate to say that he is an actor! For example, he does not want you to address him as 'Doctor' or as 'Dean' but as 'Rob,' primarily to give you the impression that he is one of the faculty and the defender of their interests, that he is first among equals, and that he does not administer by fiat but as a colleague. One day Mikha Mathias, a former member of my department, refused to submit his annual self-evaluation report on the grounds that such a report is useless, subjective, most of the time inaccurate, and practically ineffective. He discovered such lies, inaccuracies, and deception when he was on the academic council. A week after the submission date passed, the dean's secretary called Mikha and asked him to see the dean in his office on the following afternoon. He did. When he arrived, the dean left his chair and sat next to Mikha, simply to give him the impression that he was his colleague. He did not begin the meeting with the question of the self-evaluation report but with social nonsense and silly pleasantries. When this part of the meeting was over, the dean wondered about the faculty self-evaluation report. Mikha gave him logically compelling reasons for his refusal to submit a report. But the dean reminded him that he would not receive a raise if he did not submit his report. Mikha told him that he did not want to receive a raise. 'I joined the Webster faculty to teach, not to make money. Please let me know if my teaching is not satisfactory.' Then the dean reminded Mikha again that he was an employee of the college and that he should do what he was told to do. He also asked him to reconsider his decision. Mikha desisted. The dean suddenly flushed, and the flush emanated frightful anger. He stood up and said, 'Do it!' He left Mikha without saying a word and sat in his chair without looking at Mikha. Such insolence! Left alone in that lonely and dreadful silence, Mikha left the dean's office. This is the colleague King was. After Mikha reported to me what had happened in his meeting with the dean, I advised him to submit a report. He did.

"I report this encounter between Dean Beardsley and Mikha Mathias only to spotlight the fake logic, hypocrisy, and deception that will underlie Beardsley's behavior as acting president. Outwardly he and the new dean will form a search committee, will interview candidates, and will write reports to the board along with his own recommendations. The faculty will meet the candidates, and they will discuss them in a special faculty meeting. But in the end, the board will make the final decision. They give the faculty the impression that they have a say in choosing the dean or the president, they make them feel that they have a choice among two or three candidates, and then they say that the process of selecting the president or dean is a democratic process! But the question is, who selects the few candidates? The search committee? This is where the real problem lies! There is more politics than academics in this whole process, unfortunately.

"We should always remember, Stanley, that although Webster is an intellectual haven, although it upholds high standards of teaching, and although it performs a distinctive service to the city and the state, it is not an ideal work of art but aspires to be one. Oh, how naïve was that Mikha! He thought that the college was an ideal institution, not knowing that, like Socrates, he was doomed. The college is, after all, led by human beings with all their moral, intellectual, and emotional deficiencies. Perfection remains an ideal, an aspiration in human life. The dark demon lurks quietly in the hearts and minds of all human beings, even in the minds of the saints. This demon is a kind of chameleon fox! This demon rises and shows its ugly teeth the moment one's interests or survival is threatened. Those who succeed in subjugating this demon by the power of reason are few, very few."

"If, as you pointed out earlier," Dr. Lawson said, "leadership is crucial to the realization of liberal arts education, if our president and dean are not shining examples of those ideals, and if they are not wise, how can you explain the generally recognized fact that Webster is an outstanding example of higher education? What is the source of its excellence? I raise this question in spite of the fact that Webster is not an ideal work of art," Dr. Lawson asked.

"Let me first remark that positions of leadership, such as president, dean, department and division chair, are not the college. They are some of its constituents. The essential structure of the college consists of the faculty, the students, and the supporting staff. The way these constituents are related to each other and the way they function are determined by the constitution, mission statement, curriculum, quality of the faculty, traditions, practices, and general policies of the college. All these elements should exist and function as an organic unity. In their capacities as leaders, presidents, deans, chairs, and subsidiary leaders exist for one singular function: *the realization of the event of learning and, according to my view, the cultivation of character.*

"The central focus of this event is the student and the teacher. These two elements are interdependent. The teacher creates the immediate, or direct, conditions of learning, and the student is the recipient of learning,

53

assuming that growth in knowledge and understanding is the substance of learning. Neither of these two elements can exist without the other. A teacher is not a teacher without the student, and the student is not a student without the teacher. The event of learning, which shall remain unanalyzed at the present, is, I submit, the *reason for being* of the college. If you remove the reality of this event of learning, you remove the reason for being of the college, and if you undermine its significance, you undermine the significance of the college. Accordingly, a college is outstanding or mediocre inasmuch as it provides the most important conditions for the creation of an excellent event of learning. We do not judge a college as excellent because its buildings are beautiful, because it serves delicious meals to its students, because it fosters pleasant parties on weekends and special occasions, because its landscape is nice, or because the credentials of its faculty are impressive. Not at all! The pragmatic test of its excellence is the extent to which it prepares cultivated characters—morally, socially, politically, aesthetically, and personally responsible and progressive citizens."

"But," Dr. Lawson asked, "under what conditions can the event of learning or a system of such events in the different academic departments meet the conditions of excellence? Or, what makes such an event or system of events of learning excellent?"

"This is a big and intricate question, but more importantly, it is a significant question. All I can now do is give you a sketch of its fundaments, which we can discuss in some detail later."

"I understand."

"Two central conditions are necessary and, I would emphasize, indispensable for the possibility of this kind of education: first, competent teachers, and second, qualified students."

"How would you define a competent teacher and a qualified student?"

"A teacher is competent if she knows her subject, if she can communicate the subject, and if she loves her students and being a teacher. The first two requirements are intellectual and the second is moral in nature. First, the competent teacher should possess adequate and genuine knowledge of her subject. If she does not adequately know what she is teaching, if the knowledge she transmits to her students does not originate from a mind that truly understands it, regardless of whether she agrees or disagrees with the ideas she seeks to communicate, she should not be a teacher. Ideas that come from a mind that thinks clearly and adequately are more influential, more believable or understandable, than ideas that are delivered passively, impersonally. How can a student believe an idea or take it seriously if it does not come from a mind that does understand or believe it? But the primary question for us is whether the student can think about or reflect on the ideas she receives either from the teacher or from the book seriously.

"However, a teacher may be knowledgeable and she may fully understand the ideas she delivers to her students, but she may not be skilled in delivering them. Teaching is an art the way painting, sculpture, or theater is an art. Ideas signify meaning, and meaning is an inexhaustible possibility of articulation or communication in different linguistic forms and media. The teacher should be skilled in shaping and presenting her ideas in a way that enables the student to comprehend them; otherwise, they will remain foreign to the mind of the student. How can the meaning of an idea shine through the words or images the teacher communicates to the student? It is a mistake to think that difficult ideas cannot be explained or translated into simpler or more understandable language by means of analysis, analogy, illustration, explanation, or images. If meaning is formless, and it is, if the teacher comprehends a content of meaning, she should be able to form it in a way the student can comprehend it. As an artist, the teacher can use different means of communication to enable the mind of the student to comprehend.

"Moreover, a creative teacher does not deliver an already written statement or text, although the structure of the idea qua meaning already exists in her mind. She composes it in the process of delivering it. The lecture should flow from her mind the way water flows from its fountain and the way the sculpture flows from the mind of the sculptor. An artwork in process is a magical source of inspiration, understanding, and inner growth. This kind of inspiration inflames the striving of desire for knowledge and creation.

"But how can you be an artist—how can you seduce the creative impulse in your imagination, which is in no way a mean effort, in action, in front of the students if you do not respect them and treat them as growing human individuals? How can you be an artist if you are not honest not only with yourself but also with the way you communicate your ideas to your students? If our task as teachers is to communicate meaning, not stale, useless ideas; if the aim of this communication is the growth and development of the students as human beings; we can say that teaching is an activity of giving—of giving something intrinsically important. Isn't this kind of giving the essence of human love? For isn't love an act of giving of ourselves to the other regardless of whether they are family, friends, strangers, or citizens? You may charge me with extremism, if not fanaticism, if I confess to you that teaching is an act of free giving whose value cannot be assessed by material means. Yes, the teacher receives a salary at the end of the month, and the student pays a fee to the college at the beginning of the semester, which may be viewed as necessary material condition for the possibility of learning, but what actually happens in this activity is *human par excellence*. What is human cannot be measured by monetary or any other kind of value. Can you place a monetary value on love in the family, friendship, romantic relationships, helping your neighbor, or worshipping God? Can you quantitatively estimate the value of the spiritual light that flows from your mind and heart into the mind and heart of another human being?"

Dr. Lawson, who was listening attentively to his friend's response to his question, took in a deep breath and involuntarily curled his lower lip inward. It was obvious to Dr. Adams that Dr. Lawson was reflecting seriously on his remarks. He drank some water and then continued:

"Now I can move to the condition of 'qualified student.' By qualified student I mean one who is a potential learner. Let me illustrate this point by a personal example. One year, fifteen years ago, after the start of the fall semester, a female student who struck me as ambitious and bright came to my office with a drop card. 'I cannot afford to take your course, Dr. Adams.'

"'Why? Have I done something wrong?'

"'No. You require your students to think. Indeed, your course is about serious thinking. But I have no time to think deeply. I can only memorize. I am a biology and chemistry student, and I plan to go to medical school. Memorizing is what I do in my science courses.'

"'Does thinking harm you?' I asked.

"'No. It only interferes with my science studies. I need high grades. I cannot earn a high grade in your class.'

"There is no need to comment on this case, but I mention it only to emphasize that a necessary condition for the possibility of genuine learning is a desire to know, to be curious, to be willing to adventure into the world of ideas and values, and the vast sea of human experience. Not all students come to college in order to grow as human individuals, as you know. I have always hoped that at least some of my students are willing to learn. All students can learn, and they should; they are a bundle of intellectual, emotional, and imaginative potentiality. I tend to think that a caring teacher can tap this potentiality; she can stimulate in her students curiosity, and she can plant seeds of desire for knowledge in their minds. But most of all, she can inflame them with the will to grow as human individuals. Without this will, the words of the teacher will fall on deaf ears. You can take the horse to the river, but you cannot make it drink, as the ordinary saying goes. The real teacher can, I think, create an appetite for knowledge, at least the desire to know."

Dr. Adams paused for a moment with an expression of melancholy on his face and then remarked, "I know that the kind of learning I am advocating is becoming harder and harder to practice these days, not only because career-oriented education dominates a large number of our colleges as well as the mind of the young, but also because the value of liberal arts education seems to be declining in the public consciousness. I would also like to add that we are in the midst of a period of transvaluation of values. The values of pleasure, material success, and security seem to be replacing the value of happiness or human fulfillment, which is central to liberal arts education. Consumption is replacing creation; self-centeredness is replacing altruism; religious ritual is replacing religiosity; naïve individualism is replacing human community; and material success is replacing spiritual success. The human, which should be the banner under which we should conduct our lives, seems to be yielding to a herd mentality fostered by the values of the global market. This is a big issue, Stanley. I mention it in passing only because it is directly related to the survival of liberal arts education as a necessary condition for human growth and development at the individual and social levels.

"In view of what I have just said, let me now comment on the role of the leaders of the liberal arts institution—presidents, deans, chairs. If I am to use Aristotelian language, I can say that these leaders are the efficient condition of the possibility of learning as a system of events in the different departments of the college. Put differently, they exist as a means that makes this system of events possible. They may be competent or incompetent, upright or corrupt, wise or foolish; nevertheless, their role consists of enabling the faculty to ignite the fire of learning in the minds of the student. Ultimately, the faculty is the source of the light that illuminates the learning process. If the faculty is wise, competent, upright, the leader should always welcome any proposal about learning that keeps the faculty active, creative, devoted to their students, and loyal to the ideals of the college. This is exactly why no dean, no president, no chair of a department should be hired if she is not a lover of liberal arts education, if she does not believe in it, and if the spirit of liberal arts education does not animate every fiber of her mind."

"I do not simply understand your words, Seneca; I feel them. They will always remain in my mind as a gift from you." Dr. Lawson stood and kissed him on the forehead. "I shall see you tomorrow after my late afternoon lecture. We should continue this conversation."

Dr. Lawson left his friend with a heavy heart.

THREE

David Meets Eve

On the following morning, Master Death was standing exactly where he had stood and the way he had stood during his last visit when Dr. Adams opened his eyes to the world, as if the intervening time between the two visits did not exist, as if Mr. Time had taken a short excursion from the realm of being into the realm of nonbeing during that intervening period. This description may seem strange to some people because it seems impossible for Mr. Time to take a break from the realm of being! He is its essence. Someone may remind me that when time ceases to exist, reality collapses; therefore, time collapses. This is absolutely true. But this fundamental truth does not apply to Master Death because his essence is time and because he is one of the principal managers of the cosmic process. He was created simultaneously with the creation of humanity. He can take a break when he chooses. Nothing collapses during such a break; on the contrary, everything freezes when he is not active. Does time appear or in any way exist outside the cosmic process? No, because it does not exist outside the cosmic process; therefore, the question would not arise because there would not be anyone to raise it. But time is not merely a manifestation of the cosmic process. As one of its managers in the human sphere, Mr. Time is a power, one that surpasses the power of any of his ingredients such as fire, animals, or rational beings. He has a vision, an aim, and a plan to realize his aim. He adheres to his plan and does not deviate from it. He would not be able to function as Master Death if he did not have supernatural powers such as appearing and disappearing voluntarily or assuming different forms of being. Let me hasten to add that the functions he can perform are neither capricious nor erratic. They are determined by a carefully designed plan. Like everything that exists, including the cosmic process, he is a creature, and as a creature he is limited by the laws according to which he was created. For example, although he is not a human being, he can act as one because he is superior to them in power and intelligence, and although he is not like the creatures that make up the structure of the cosmic process, he can appear in any form he chooses and act according to the essence of that form. If I am to characterize him briefly, I can say that he is an incarnation, or concrete embodiment, of one aspect of the essence of time.

A little later I shall try to show that Master Death has a special interest in human beings, in those who conduct their lives from the standpoint of their humanity. Dr. Adams is one of those beings. By the way, existentially, not all people conduct their lives from the standpoint of the human essence, at least not consciously, not on principle, and not completely. For example, many of them behave like members of a herd of sheep, contrary to their essence, and feel satisfied with this way of life; many of them drift as human beings; and many of them lead a mediocre way of life. Most of them live with the knowledge that they will die, but they do not know what it means to die, or to live on the basis of that knowledge. They deny by the way they live the existence or even significance of death. Master Death ignores those people; for him, they do not even live. But he gets angry, roweled up, when a genuine human being such as Dr. Adams denies the existence of death, which means he denies the existence of Master Death. He thinks that a human being who denies his existence is a blatant contradiction. How could he deny the existence of death if Master Death exists? This kind of contradiction stares him in the eyes as a formidable challenge. But what can he do about it? Can he meet this challenge? It may seem at first look that this master is vain, arrogant, and imperious, but is he? Is he simply trying to assert his legitimate supremacy? Nevertheless, he tends to think that the majority of the human species misunderstand him, and he is anxious to reverse this tendency, especially among those who understand.

At first, Dr. Adams could not tell whether the figure that met his eyes when he opened them to the world was an apparition or maybe the same strange being who had visited him yesterday, but that very figure had come to his rescue. "I am Master Death!" he said. "I thought that you would like to see me rather than your nurse or your dear friend Dr. Lawson." A frown suddenly knotted itself on Dr. Adams's forehead. It was a tense, admonishing frown. He could not speak only because his throat was dry.

His jaw twitched a little. The medications he had taken during the night must have been the cause of this dryness. The water pitcher was on the side table next to his bed. He filled a glass, drank some, and then stared at his uninvited guest with a feeling of disappointment. His head was not yet clear. He craved a cup of coffee at that moment. "Coffee and along with it your breakfast are on their way to your room," the uninvited guest said without moving his vitreous eyes from Dr. Adams's face. And in fact, the rack of food trays stopped at the door of his room at that moment. Dr. Adams could not conjecture whether the arrival of the rack was by design or whether it had arrived according to its regular schedule.

"Good morning!" the rack lady said cheerfully, interrupting the interchange between Dr. Adams and Master Death. "The eggs are scrambled and the potatoes are baked, as you requested," she said in a friendly, cheerful voice. "Enjoy!" she added without acknowledging the presence of the guest. But she could not help noticing his pale face, stony cheeks, and lifeless eyes. She did not have the right words to express the feeling she experienced when she noticed him. How can you have a definable reaction to a faceless face? The rack lady awkwardly turned her eyes away from him, focused them on Dr. Adams, and said, "I wish you a pleasant day, Dr. Adams!" and in the silence of her mind she added, "You will need it!" She left the room hurriedly.

Still in a rather tense mood, Dr. Adams darted a sharp look at the stranger and asked sternly, "Who are you? What right do you have to intrude into my privacy? I demand an answer to my question; otherwise, I request that you leave my presence immediately!"

"There is no need to be agitated, Dr. Adams. You are well known for your prudence and especially for your temperance. Please do not allow your emotions to constrict your patience. I cannot lie, even if I try. I am always myself. This is how I was created. Deception, hypocrisy, deviousness, and trickery are human qualities. I am not human. I cannot be. Your friend is one of its passing shadows. All those who are mushy lovers are accidents. They are cowards. They hide in the shadow of love, but real love does not know them nor can it recognize them. True lovers are courageous, adventurers: they are creators. Neither wind, snow, sleet, nor fire stands in their way. They are meteorites of the divine—the ideal of the artist and the aspiration of the sage. True lovers are givers. They give freely without knowing that they give. Giving is their essence. They thrive on their own creation. They do not know how to receive. They feel embarrassed, even guilty, if someone tries to give them something they deserve, even honor. On the contrary, honor is never on their mind. They give honor; they do not receive it. Oh, your friend is pitiful—your kind of pity, of course—because he receives, and he receives because he has a desire to receive. He thrives on your love and respect. Show me true friends united by the bond of true love and I show you the divine. But this kind of friendship does not exist. True friends are united by the radiance of their creation, not by the need for security and certainly not by the need to receive—support, knowledge, something material. I do not wish to hurt your feelings, Dr. Adams. I cannot because I do not know how. I do not have the capacity of feeling, and I do not have the capacity of desiring. How can I hurt your feelings if I do not have the capacity to feel?

"I am on a mission, and I intend to fulfill it."

Dr. Adams, whose chest was heaving heavily, shook his head. The more he listened to him, the more he was struck by the versatility of the stranger. A storm of conflicting emotions and ideas gushed into his mind and heart. Truly he was confused. He was torn between two clashing streams of consciousness. On the one hand, he was impressed by the soundness of the stranger's logic and knowledge of human beings, and, on the other hand, he was repelled by his biting coldness, his abnormal superpowers, which Dr. Adams could not believe, and the stranger's outrageous claim that he was Master Death, which was impossible for Adams to believe. *Death does not exist*, he thought, and yet the ghastly appearance of the stranger, despite the fact that he was nicely dressed, and his abrasive behavior seemed to emanate from a being who had just risen from the dead or had just broken loose from Homer's Hades. When he was at Webster, Dr. Adams applied the Socratic method of teaching. The guiding principle of his method was reason. He always believed that if we analyze a question, a problem, or an intricate concept logically, we should sooner or later arrive at an answer to the question or problem or a clear articulation of the concept. His immediate impulse at that juncture of his encounter with the stranger was to question him. He was convinced that this was the most appropriate way to remove the mask the stranger was wearing, if he was wearing one. But regardless of whether he was wearing a mask, the truth would in some way be discovered. Dr. Adams did not know the personal identity of his students when he used to teach. He interacted with them on the assumption that they were learners. Why not interact with this intruder on the same assumption? He might or might not have been truthful or genuine in his claim that he was Master Death and that he was not a human being. Dr. Adams believed that logical analysis would reveal the truth. But what if the stranger were an actor, or a mischievous actor? Frankly, Dr. Adams did not take this possibility seriously. He was, as the stranger recognized, a courageous human being.

"Oh, Dr. Adams! I told you who I am. You do not seem to believe me. Again, let me assure you that I am Master Death. I am the reality of death itself; I am its quintessence. If you grasp my essence, you grasp the essence of death."

"Such a reality does not exist. Who are you? Speak!"

"But it does exist. You think it does not only because you are a prisoner to your own logic—to human logic. You cannot conceive the possibility of another logic because your mind does not possess the categories and the necessary relations by which you and rest of human beings think. Without these categories and relations, you cannot discern the higher and broader logical relations of the things you try to conceive or try to understand. For example, Janice will come to this room within two minutes and attend to you with the utmost loving respect. She will inform you that Dr. Hardy, who is absolutely certain that your life is very short, believes that a man of your high moral, intellectual, and aesthetic endowments, a man who has given so generously to the college, a luminary in the state of Mississippi, should not die. He loves you, and he will sing praises of love for you. Unlike many of your students, he will acknowledge his success as a human being and as a scientist to you and will express a deep feeling of gratitude to you. He is not a poet, but he will try to express his feelings poetically. But this time Janice will not see me because I shall vanish before she lays her eyes on me. I do not like her. She cares for you, and she would fall in love with you if you were a little younger, not because she is a source of love but because she craves to be loved. Such people are feeble, beggars; they stimulate the sour juices of my being. I hate these juices! I understand her, but she cannot understand me. Like the majority of people, she cannot understand the meaning of the word, much less the reality of death."

"But—" Dr. Adams tried to defend the nurse and the important service she rendered to her patients, but the stranger interrupted him.

"I understand your loyalty to her and to all the people you respect," the stranger said. "You should first let me assure you that, now in a different way, that I am Master Death; I am real, as real as the reality of your sickly body and everything around you." And with a sarcastic grin in the corner of his mouth, he added, "I am more real than the reality of any living human being. Please do not interrupt me." Dr. Adams remained silent reluctantly, but the stranger felt his reluctance. "I mean well, Dr. Adams. You may think that I am insulting you, but I am not. You do not believe that I am Master Death, that I am real, and that death is real. By the authority of what logic, what line of reasoning, do you doubt my claims? How can you allow this doubt to even enter your mind if you are talking to me now? The fact of your doubt, and it is a fact, is an explicit assertion, affirmation, that I am real. But if my present conversation with you is real, then call me Mr. Conversation since you cannot deny the facticity of this conversation. But can you, according to your own logic, conduct a conversation without a subject that conducts it?" The stranger paused for a moment and cast a sarcastic look at Dr. Adams.

"You are toying with words. I have no desire to indulge in sophistic nonsense—

"Logic rejects your pretensions. The notion that death can assume a human form and communicate with people is a mythical notion. Undeveloped minds, minds that cannot provide rational explanation to what seems mysterious or difficult to understand, reify and humanize the forces and causes that underlie what they cannot explain, and they tend to endow them with supernatural power. Would you please refrain from sophistry and deception? Death does not exist and it cannot converse with anyone because it is not a reality. You are real to me; you are conversing with me; therefore, you are not what you say you are. Who are you? What is your purpose, or mission, if you really have one?"

"We shall continue this conversation. We must! I shall be the one who conducts my explanations and arguments with you, not Mr. Conversation."

The stranger vanished, and Janice entered the room, showing the liveliest smile on her face. She was a radiance of gladness. "Good morning!" she said. "How is my patient this morning?"

"I am doing well, my dear," Dr. Adams said, trying to subdue the unpleasant mood the stranger had provoked in his mind a few minutes ago.

"But you have not eaten your breakfast!" she said as she was moving closer to his bed. She pushed the side table closer to his chest and removed the cover off his coffee cup. "How about some coffee?"

"Excellent idea! Yes please," he responded enthusiastically. "Thank you!"

Dr. Adams took a big sip of coffee which he needed badly, and said, "How are you doing this morning, Janice?"

"This morning I feel very glad. I have good news for you. Dr. Hardy will see you a little later. He thinks that your condition is relatively stable and it will remain stable during the following several days. He evaluated your chart and came to the conclusion that it might be appropriate for you to spend the next few days at home. This will give you a greater measure of privacy and freedom. I really feel that this is a most welcome news."

"Yes, it is," Dr. Adams said thoughtfully in the silence of his mind and added, "Some people might think that it is a gift, a kind of bonus, and they might think I should be lucky to be granted this kind of gift. But I wonder! Does it matter whether this gift is a few hours, a few days, a few weeks, or more? I have fulfilled my destiny in this world."

"No, you have not, not yet!" a voice surging from the depth of his being into his consciousness said. Every moment of life in which you can promote the well-being of one human being, hopefully more, is an integral part of your destiny. You cannot extricate yourself from this obligation with impunity."

Dr. Adams sank into a pensive state of mind involuntarily. *But what kind of good can I promote in this state of body and mind? Whose good can I promote?*

"Your friends, your students, and your mere presence in this world—your presence is an embodiment of the highest human values. These values are rays of light; such rays should remain shining as long as possible. Light is good; you cannot undermine the good! Can you underestimate the value of your presence? Can you underestimate the value of the human as such?" the same voice responded but could not continue its response only because Janice, who had noticed this sudden change in his mood, intervened.

"Dr. Adams, are you in pain?" she asked, alarmed.

"I am just fine, Janice," he responded. "Once in a while, strange ideas visit me. Sometimes they are friendly, and at other times they are grouchy. I am used to their sudden visits. Do not worry, please. They are just ideas. Ideas do not harm."

"You have to eat!" she said.

"Yes, I have to. Frankly, I am hungry."

"Good! I shall be back shortly."

The pensive mood that had surprised Dr. Adams a little while ago returned. The question that was written on its front was a question with which he had struggled many times when he was analyzing the possibility of human life in general and moral life in particular: Can a human being take a break from moral action, from the obligation to act morally every moment of her life, that is, from thinking, feeling, and acting morally? Is this kind of life possible, or is it simply an ideal? It would seem that if we deviate from this way of thinking, feeling, and acting, we would betray ourselves as human beings because being moral is an essential condition of being human. It is difficult to conceive the human without conceiving the moral as one of its essential ingredients. Again, can we be moral if we do not choose to be moral? Should every activity of ours, regardless of its kind, emanate from a moral will, from a moral heart?

But the voice spoke again. "Yes, every activity, even moments of pleasure, sadness, rest, or some kind of entertainment should emanate from a moral will because this will kind of will requires them. If you are moral, then you as a whole would be moral. Everything you do has in some way some serious implications on the life of other people and on what you will next."

"What about the condition of choice?"

"When you have chosen your vocation, you have also chosen your way of life. Practically, your life revolves around your vocation. It is a center in terms of which you design your plans and make decisions about all the aspects of your family, social, and professional activities. Your life is an organic whole. Accept it as a whole. Your vocation is its axis," the voice said.

"You seem to assume that a human being can lead a human way of life until the last moment of her existence. But people get old, they get weak, and they see the world and experience it with new or different eyes and minds. Are they under obligation to act morally until the last second of their lives?"

"Yes, to the very end."

"What if their will weakens and their desire loses its enthusiasm for life?"

"They cannot choose to shrink from their moral heart. They may make mistakes, but they cannot will from a nonmoral heart."

"You strike me as austere, excessively austere."

"Any object that acts according to its essence or nature completely can never be austere?"

"I am not sure," Dr. Adams said pensively.

"Don't you think that one should lead a human way of acting, or to use your language, a creative, constructive way of acting, to the very end?"

"So far as she can. Except when the body is incapacitated and obstructs the activity of the mind, the human being should, in principle and to some extent, act creatively, constructively. You are approaching your end, you are taking strong tranquilizers, and you are succumbing to lung and heart attacks, and yet you are conducting some of the most important conversations with your friends and students, and you frequently conduct these conversations in the midst of severe pain."

"Let me remind you of an idea you discussed in one of your lectures on the value of human life. The proposition you defended is that human life is sacred—correct?"

"Yes, I did."

"But if it is sacred, can we neglect it as long as we can live it?"

"No."

"Even when we reach the very end? Let me at once remind you of how Socrates was willing and able to give one of his students a good lesson in moral behavior even when he was dying, and of how the Roman philosopher Seneca died willingly and valiantly."

"But can we treat our life as sacred, and can we love it, if we do not act productively as long as we live it? Let me ask one more time, Can we shrink from our duties even when we approach the end? For example, can we lie, cheat, or betray our friends when we are bidding them the final goodbye? I tend to think that if we take a break from moral action even when we approach the end, we undermine the sanctity of the life we have lived and the dignity of the human beings we loved; in short, we reveal to the world that the life we led was sham."

"The dignity of human beings?"

"Yes. We can ask, what is the source of dignity but acting according to the values that define our humanity? Aren't moral values central to the texture of this humanity?"

"I understand your explanation of the basis of human dignity, but I am skeptical about your assertion that one can lead a creative, productive life until the last moment of her life. The source of my skepticism is not whether a person can be productive or creative when she reaches the last station of her life but the possible realization, one that frequently visits us when we reach our mature years, whether this very creative and productive life was worth the trouble we went through to achieve it. What if a person stands before the wall people call death; what if she looks back at her life and contemplates it; what if she realizes that the impending end is the very end, that this end is the door to nonbeing; what if she recognizes that this means the end of everything for her, that she and what she achieved would soon sink into the world of nonbeing; or what if she realizes that in fact the moral palace she designed and built would splinter into fragments of nothing; and then what if she compares how she struggled and suffered to build that palace to how most of the people around her did not give a hoot about morality but nevertheless led, and continue to lead, an enjoyable life—yes, how should this moral idealist, this noble soul feel? Let me illustrate this point, which has been pricking my brain for some time now, by a conversation I had with my teacher, mentor, and friend shortly after I completed my graduate studies.

"My teacher was a flame of creative, productive life. He was a devoted scholar, teacher, and minister of a church. As far as I know, he was a truly moral human being, moral to the core. He was struck by cancer in his late sixties. He endured it for a while. When he reached the end, he lost his appetite for life. He was about to finish a book about the foundation of religion, but when the shadow of death loomed clearly in the sphere of his consciousness, he stopped writing, he threw away all the books and articles he had written, and he fell into deep silence until the moment of his death. I visited him. He embraced me in silence when he saw me. He used to be a radiance of smiles and ideas about philosophy and especially about social justice, but now he spent his time staring into an indefinable space—his own space. 'It has been a vain battle!' he told me in a moment of self-composure when we were walking in the park on the following afternoon.

"'What do you mean?' I inquired.

"'It--' he said without completing his sentence. I waited for a few seconds, hoping that he would complete his sentence, but instead he gazed into the infinity of his own space, the space of his inner world.

"'What does "it" refer to?' I asked timidly.

"'All . . . '

"'All what?' I inquired again with a deeper feeling of timidity.

"'My life'—he paused for a moment and added, 'and this whole spectacle you call world. Nothing! All is nothing—from nothing into nothing.'

"'And the life we live—is it nothing?'

"He did not answer, but he added affirmatively, dejectedly, cynically, 'Are you different from or better than the rock, the tree, the bird, or the bug? The tree is a living organism. It endures for a while, and then it passes away. So does every object that exists. Every object endures for a certain period according to its nature and then ceases to exist. The primary difference between us and the rest of creation is that we are conscious of the world around us, we know that the world exists, and we are conscious of ourselves. Our problem is that we possess self-consciousness. This spectacle you call world is nothing but a show most people view as reality, but it is not. This cursed nothing is all that exists; the world is its shadow.'

"'Are you sure?'

"'Does God the Father exist?'

"I frowned when I heard that unexpected question. It took me a few seconds to see its meaning and implications. 'Of course not. Even the popes, the patriarchs, and the bishops do not anymore believe in his existence.'

"'If God the Father does not exist, then the power of nothing governs the cosmic process. But again, reality abides; therefore, what does not abide does not really exist. Like the world we seem to enjoy, our life is an ongoing show, the face of nothing.'

"'What does the idea of God the Father have to do with our reality or its meaning?' I asked only because I knew that he had been a deeply religious man.

"'If God the Father exists, he should be the Creator, and as the Creator, he should be in charge of what he creates. Again, he cannot be such a source if he does not abide eternally, if he does not give meaning to the life he creates. I have striven to build all my life according to his will, but he does not exist. The same applies to any meaning we create or live by. Those who speak of ideals and absolute values, ideals and values that are universal or eternal, assume the existence of some God-the-Father being; otherwise, such ideals and values are human creations. But like everything human and natural, nothing endures. All comes from the belly of nothing and ends up in it! The ancient Greeks and Romans were more honest, more realistic, mor human than we are in this glorious West!'

"'But we create meaning out of nothing—'

"He chuckled! 'You create it, and then it dies with you. Do not be misled by Plato's and Whitehead's concept of objective immortality. This is only an interesting idea, a sedative that keeps you going and prevents you from committing suicide. The meaning you create is part and parcel of your being, which is a passing ripple in the cosmic process.'"

Master Death and Janice had been correct. Dr. Hardy, surrounded by a retinue of nurses—Janice, two nurses, and three students—left the nurses' station after he had studied Dr. Adams's chart and explained to them the patient's condition. A waft of seriousness, of something important, moved from the nurses' station to Dr. Adams's room. Dr. Hardy was one of the most distinguished scientists, professors, and surgeons at the School of Medicine. Whatever he did or said, wherever he went, he generated an air of importance. Both his face and demeanor radiated thoughtfulness, importance. Even the students and nurses who surrounded him wore an expression of seriousness and importance. It was an honor to hear Dr. Hardy speak, perform surgery, or deliver a lecture.

Dr. Adams's eyes were gazing at the blue sky through the open window of his room when the commotion created by the entrance of the robust team of medical experts aborted that gaze. He must have been deeply interested in the sky and especially in its blue face. No one could conjecture whether he was reflecting on his conversation with the voice or whether he was having a mystical experience with the Infinite, for which he was famous. But Dr. Adams was the kind of human being who shunned idleness. He simply did not know how to be idle. Idleness necessarily entailed killing time, but killing time was tantamount to killing a portion of one's life; therefore, it would be wrong to be idle. Undermining one's life was immoral, he thought. His mind was always on the go, so to say, but it did not dwell on the petty or the mediocre. It was made to struggle with the difficult questions of human life, those questions that relate to the essence of things. For him, an inquiry into the essence of an object, regardless of whether it be the cosmos, the atom, or human destiny, and advancing our understanding of it was a significant service to humanity.

It was obvious to Dr. Hardy, who was quite familiar with Dr. Adams's life and work, that his patient was having a conversation with the inner voice of the universe, a secret not many people at Webster knew about him. Dr. Hardy was kind, modest, and generous. It took Dr. Adams a few seconds to recover from that conversation. When you inhabit two worlds that are different in their being and constitution, and when you are a loyal citizen of both words, it is not easy to move from one to the other.

"Good morning, Professor Adams!" Dr. Hardy spoke with a warm voice. Dr. Adams smiled and stretched his hand to Dr. Hardy, who received it with a firm but friendly shake. "These wonderful people would like to inquire about you. All of us want to know how you are feeling."

Dr. Adams cast a curious, appreciative look at the nurses and then at the doctor. "No one in my position can have the right words to express my feeling of gratitude to these caring and lovely ladies. I only wish I could communicate my feeling actively, not merely verbally. I tend to think that they are God's healing hands on earth. I truly hope that society in general and our society in particular can recognize this fact in a meaningful way both materially and morally. But they, especially you, Dr. Hardy, know my condition more than anyone in our community. These ladies are not only nurses of the body but also of the tired soul, especially the soul that is about to leave the world. Only a generous, loving, self-denying person can nurse a human being in my state." Dr. Adams paused, had a sip of water, embraced the nurses with a compassionate look, and then added, "As to how I am now feeling, all I can say is that I am content, more gratified than content."

When he was speaking, the eyes of the nurses glittered with interest. One of them bit her lower lip and blushed. The head nurse tried to swallow whatever saliva was in her mouth. The third nurse was so tense she frowned with a deep feeling of seriousness, and Janice suppressed a flood of tears that was about to burst out of her eyes. They and many others did not know that Dr. Hardy knew that he was Professor Adams's student, and they did not know that the illustrious Dr. Hardy was an aesthetically refined mind.

"You must be a magician, Professor Adams!" Dr. Hardy said lovingly.

"A magician?" Dr. Adams responded with a chuckle.

"Let me express my point differently—charming? For example, Janice vehemently insisted that she would be your nurse. Can this kind of loyalty be fortuitous?"

"How can a shriveled old man on his way out of the realm of being be charming?"

"Charm is not a mere function of the body, and it is not causally related to it. Beauty and goodness do not age, as you insisted more than once in your lectures in the aesthetics course when I was your student at Webster. They are brilliant, eternally youthful. They resist aging. Therefore, a youthful or old person can be charming—correct?"

"But—"

Dr. Hardy did not allow his teacher to continue. "One day spent with a charming person is better than a lifetime spent with a dull, crass, boring person. Charm is indifferent to age. An old person can be elegant exactly the way a young person can be elegant. Charm, or elegance, is a jewel that

71

shines from within. These are your exact words, Professor Adams. You are this kind of jewel."

The nurses' eyes were instantly directed, as though by a magnet, toward Dr. Hardy's face. They emanated astonishment and interest.

"But am I the person you are talking about, James?" asked Dr. Adams.

"You are! I am not the only witness, and I am not the only judge! You may leave us, and you will leave us soon, but the shimmer of your charm will linger in my heart and the hearts of many students who attended your classes."

Dr. Hardy did not give his former teacher a chance either to speak or to respond to his remarks. He, like most of the Webster community, knew Dr. Adams's modesty, generosity, and austere self-consciousness. He thought that the complimentary remarks he communicated were final and resisted any doubt or discussion. He lowered his body toward Adams's face and kissed him on the forehead. "I shall see you soon, dear teacher. In the meantime, Janice will tend to your medical needs."

Amazed and speechless, the nurses followed Dr. Hardy as he marched out of the room rather serenely. It was not easy for Dr. Hardy, and especially the nurses, to recover their self-composure immediately.

This short visit had been an extraordinary experience for the nurses. The gulf that usually separated doctors, and especially scientists, and their assistants is usually wide, as if each belongs to a different world or speaks a different language. It is difficult to give an adequate explanation of this fact. Is it because doctors can prolong human life, which is supremely dear to people? But Dr. Hardy was firmly convinced that this gulf should not exist. Whether consciously or unconsciously, he exemplified this belief in the way he interacted with his former teacher, who was a highly and widely recognized philosopher. In a way, this kind of gulf seems to exist between any expert and the assistants that revolve in her orbit. For her, all people are equal in her humanity.

Regardless of whether a person is an artist, businessperson, biologist, engineer, or farmer, she deserves special respect, reward, or consideration inasmuch as she fulfills her potential or vocation in life distinctively. I do not respect a person simply because she is a doctor, a farmer, an artist, or an engineer, or because she is a proficient doctor, artist, engineer, or farmer, but especially because she is a good human being, and she is a good human being when she acts morally and when she serves society according to her talents proficiently. How many a student despises a teacher because she is incompetent or corrupt? How many a person frowns indignantly at a politician, inventor, lawyer, or businessperson because she is incompetent morally and professionally? On the other hand, don't we admire and respect and honor a soldier, a nurse, or a secretary who acts morally as a person and skillfully as a professional?

Dr. Adams was napping when Dr. Lawson came to visit him late that morning. He sat on a chair at the foot of his friend's bed and decided to wait until his friend opened his eyes to the light of the day. But he did not wait for long because Janice came in with a box of medications Dr. Hardy had prescribed. She was very glad to see Dr. Lawson. After they exchanged the usual morning greetings, she informed him that Dr. Hardy had paid a heartwarming visit to Dr. Adams and that Dr. Adams would spend the next few days at his home tomorrow. "This does not mean," Janice added, "that Dr. Adams will heal in the near or distant future; it only means that he will be happier at home than in this dreary room. Dr. Adams's comfort is uppermost in Dr. Hardy's mind. He is doing his utmost to prolong his life and to make sure that it is comfortable and meaningful." She paused for a second, a reflective second, and added, "This is the first time any of us here in this wing of the hospital have clearly witnessed the human side of Dr. Hardy—a very impressive person. He may strike some people as aloof, distant, but he is a big bundle of human feeling and a distinctive personification of modesty. He is the kind who leads without being a leader. Have you met him?"

"No, but I have heard much about his scientific achievements—a great mind."

Janice's phone rang. She had to leave, but before leaving, she said that she would return shortly because she had to administer the new medication to Dr. Adams. Dr. Lawson returned to his chair and waited, but the wait was not long because Dr. Adams slowly opened his eyes, not to the dim light of the room but to the luminous face of his friend. He smiled, and his smile was met with a "good morning!" Dr. Lawson turned on the light and brought his chair closer to the right side of the bed.

"How do you feel, Seneca?"

"I cannot tell you exactly how I feel because I am under the influence of some drugs, but I can say that I am thankful for being able to think and communicate with my dear friend. Tell me, how is your work, Stanley?"

"My work is fine but not the work of your former department."

"Why?"

"Some of the faculty are worried about the young Mitzakis. A number of students complained about his accent. Some of them said that it is hard to understand him, and others complained that he is a foreigner."

"But I heard that his English is excellent."

"Yes, but for some, if you do not speak with a southern accent, you do not speak English."

"I did not expect this kind of reaction." Dr. Adams fell into a momentary reverie, at the end of which he uttered two words: "Ignorance! Prejudice!" Then he added, "This is a main reason that liberal arts education is urgently needed in our society. It is one of the strongest forces that promotes tolerance, harmony, justice, and the freedom we prize in our political system. Intellectual and cultural enlightenment are necessary conditions for social harmony and human progress."

"I heard that the main topic the dean plans to present for discussion at the next meeting is the mission statement we should envision as a faculty. He thinks that the statement should take into consideration recent economic and political developments."

"How is the work of your committee going?"

"Disastrously!"

"What is happening?"

"This is why the mission statement will be the only topic for discussion at the next meeting this afternoon. In addition to some reference to economic and technological developments, the dean wants the statement to reflect the curricular changes he envisions—"

"What kind of changes does he envision?"

"The exact changes desired are not crystal clear yet, but their general drift is toward changing the humanities part of the curriculum from a survey- and history-oriented to a topic-oriented curriculum. The chair of the political science department is critical of this proposal. He sent me a copy of his reaction. It might be useful if I read it to you. He plans to present it for discussion at a forthcoming faculty meeting. Let me read his remarks to you:

"'When Webster changed its core curriculum a couple of years ago, required courses such as English Comp, Soph. Lit, Western Civ, both Old and New Testament, and many others were abolished. Except for students taking Heritage, requirements were transformed into topic curses that were specifically not survey courses. The following analysis by me indicates what a student can take to meet graduate requirements.

Curriculum Choices That Satisfy Webster Core 2–5

A student who selects to take these 2–5 courses can satisfy the Webster Arts & Letters Core without being exposed to Greek and Roman civilization, most of the Old Testament and all of the New, Charlemagne, the (European) Renaissance, Shakespeare (or anything that occurred in Europe from 1500 to 1800). *And this is a liberal education?*

Core 2

Creation Stories of the Ancient World. An analysis of the creation stories in their cultural contexts from peoples of the ancient world, with special consideration of the beliefs that are expressed through their literature and artistic creations, and that give coherence to their common life. Focus: Religion.

Core 3

Life in a Time of Death: Bubonic Plague and the Cult of Death. A consideration of the bubonic plague in the mid-1300s as a historical event that greatly affected religious, intellectual, artistic, economic, and social life. Particular attention will be given to literary treatments of the Black Death. Parallels will be drawn with more recent epidemics, such as the 1918 flu epidemic and AIDS. Focus: Literature and History.

Core 4

Wagner's Tristan and Isolde: A Metaphor of Romanticism. How artistic and philosophical ideas of the nineteenth century coalesce in Wagner's compelling and controversial masterpiece. The opera will provide the lens through which various aspects of romanticism will be viewed. Focus: Fine Arts.

Core 5

Images of the South in the Contemporary World. A study of the Southern Renaissance (1920–1950) as seen by historians, writers, and photographers; an investigation of the evolving and shifting portraits they have provided;

and an examination of southern history and literature in the context of Modernism as a worldwide intellectual movement. Focus: Literature.

"What do you think, Seneca?"

"I cannot answer your question adequately because changing the curriculum of a college such as Webster involves an analysis of intricate questions, values, assumptions, and traditions, which I cannot now do, but I can make some remarks that can be used as a basis for a reasonable answer. You can call them general guidelines. We can discuss them in some detail in the following few days, hopefully before I leave the world. I shall begin with two sets of remarks. The first is historical, and the second is philosophical.

"First, the basic structure of the new curriculum the dean and his cronies on your and the curriculum revision committees undermines the cultivation of historical consciousness in the mind of the student, which is a necessary condition for understanding any problem, phenomenon, development, or achievement. No one of the proposed topics and no topic that centers on a problem or phenomenon in any area of human knowledge can be understood apart from a comprehensive analysis or consideration of the economic, political, religious, social, and cultural institutions or developments that take place in a given cultural and historical context, and we cannot understand a historical period by analyzing it simply or primarily, because the life of a society in its historical context as a process is an organically interrelated system of events. We cannot understand the nature and dynamics of any part of the system without understanding the system as an organic whole, as a whole in process. How can we understand any part if we do not have a clear idea of the context? But any context is an integral part of an ongoing historical process. Can we understand any problem or phenomenon if we do not understand the historical dynamics that gave rise to the problem or phenomenon? The mere study of the problem does not inform us of the historical context in which it occurred. Can I make an inference about the historical period in which the bubonic plague occurred merely by a study of this event? No. Can I understand the meaning of the plague outside its historical period? No.

"Moreover, focus on a topic raises the question of subjectivism. What if the teachers who design a core course are inept pedagogically, and what if they are ideologically, religiously, philosophically, or culturally biased or oriented? What criteria or standards can we use to evaluate the adequacy of their design? Nowadays we live in pluralistic and frequently conflicting ideological, religious, political, and cultural ways of thinking and living.

Can the designers of core courses be prejudice or bias free? If you remove historical consciousness and historical knowledge, you also remove the possibility of an objective basis of a coherent, tested, and authoritative liberal arts education.

"The authors of the revised curriculum commit what is known as the fallacy of misplaced concreteness. They abstract an element of a whole from its context and focus their exclusive attention on it, thinking that the student will, by a process of intellectual osmosis or by a magical act of the imagination, comprehend the whole whose comprehension is a necessary condition for understanding the part.

"What is even worse, Stanley, is that the student will not 'know,' or even have an idea, of the history of human civilization. But this knowledge is a necessary condition for understanding the fabric of the forces that underlie a given historical period. For example, how can we understand the Byzantine period or culture if we do not know the Hellenistic period, and how can we understand the Hellenistic period if we do not know the Hellenic period? And how can we understand the Hellenic period if we do understand the Homeric period?

"The principle of explanation I have just illustrated applies to our understanding of any institution, achievement, event, or rise of genius in any practical or theoretical sphere of our life. Can we understand the art or an artist of ancient Greece or that of the Middle Ages apart from the political, economic, military, religious, and social context within which the art movement or artist flourished? Can we understand the rise of a man such as Plato, Galileo, Newton, or Shakespeare apart from an understanding of the whole cultural context of the period in which he flourished? History of the world is history of human civilization, and this history is an organically developing process. An understanding of any part of this process is incomplete if we do not attempt to understand it as a part of the whole of which it is a part. Again, can we adequately understand the rise and development of the USA as a world power if we do not understand the general history of Europe, which is an integral part of world history? Although the founders of the state were American citizens and patriots, they were historically minded; they were versatile in the history of ancient Greece and Rome and modernity, and they incorporated some of their basic beliefs and values in conceiving the vision that underlies the creation and growth of the US constitution. Can we understand American civilization without an understanding of its roots, and how can we understand how these roots grew in the march of history? A historically minded individual thinks from the standpoint of the history of the world or from the standpoint of a historical epoch.

"Second, let me remind you of an important conclusion we reached in a previous conversation on liberal arts education. We have seen that the primary aim of this kind of education is cultivation of character. The point is to enable the student to grow and develop as a human individual. How can a college such as Webster pursue this aim? A discussion of the basic structure of human character should begin with an understanding of the structure of human nature because the structure of human nature is the basis and source of human character: the fabric of human character is made up of the human dimension of human beings.

"Now, human nature is made up of four basic capacities or powers: thinking, which aims at the value of truth; feeling, which aims at the value of goodness and beauty; willing, which aims at the value of freedom or self-determination; and creation, which aims at the value of personal and professional development. Any discourse about the value of the human as such is in the final analysis a discourse about one or a combination of these capacities. The unity of these capacities makes up the fabric of human character. When we refer to a human being as a seasoned or strong character, we usually mean that her capacities of thinking, feeling, willing, and creation are developed and refined. But the question we are trying to answer is, How can Webster College promote the cultivation of the character of the student?"

"An excellent point!"

"The cultivation process begins when the child is born and reaches a significant degree of development toward the end of her adolescence, around her graduation from high school. In principle, this is a lifelong process. We may say that a reasonable measure of development is a necessary condition for the kind of cultivation that takes place at Webster. The task of liberal arts education is to initiate the student into the infinite world of philosophy, art, science, morality, politics, religion, and social life; to make her cognizant of her own intellectual, artistic, social, religious, political, and creative powers; to expose her to the central questions of existence in general and human existence in particular; and especially to show her how to live, that is, how to love, desire, establish a family, make sound decisions, and embark on a meaningful life. This view is based on the fundamental assumption that knowledge is a means to human living. The end is, as we argued earlier, living well, always better."

"But then, how does, or should, Webster enable its students to embark on this most important adventure of their lives?" Dr. Lawson asked.

"By creating the kind of theoretical and practical conditions that activate the human capacities that exist in their minds as potentialities and open the fountain of the desire for human growth and development—of the desire to know, to appreciate the beautiful, to do good, to make sound decisions, and to become the human individuals they should be. The kind of liberal arts education I envision should be transformative in character—"

"Transformative?" Dr. Lawson asked, interrupting his friend. "In what sense?"

"In the sense that every student undergoes, regardless of whether theoretical or existential, an experience that makes a difference in the way she thinks, feels, wills, and succeeds in making the serious decisions of her life. This kind of experience is constructive, additive, accumulative in nature because it expands the depth and breadth of the cognitive, affective, and imaginative powers of the mind. In this kind of experience, the mind does not remain passive; it becomes active, creative. It discerns the truth, beauty, and goodness of an object or situation for what it is, assents to it and incorporates the truth in its own mind. It becomes a part of the cognitive, affective, and vital powers of the mind. What the mind incorporates in this experience ceases to be 'an other' or a strange reality because it understands and receives it according to its cognitive vision and understanding. This type of incorporation is the essence of human development. To develop as a human being is essentially to expand—to enlarge or deepen—our capacities of seeking the truth, appreciating the beautiful, and making sound judgments."

"Do you think that this vision of liberal arts education is realistic? Is this what is happening in the different classrooms at Webster College?"

"We have no right to judge the kinds of experiences that are being created in the different classrooms of the college. Our only indicators are students' reports and confessions. We may also survey the number of our graduates who assume distinguished positions of leadership in the state and the nation. If I were to take these sources of information seriously, I feel a bit pessimistic; my pessimism has deepened during the past few years."

"Why?"

"For the same reason that prompted the president and his dean to change the curriculum and the whole philosophy of the college."

"The whole philosophy of the college?"

"Yes."

"How?"

"Dr. Hammond, the president, first asked a committee to study the existing curriculum and the way it is implemented in the different academic departments? Has he asked such a committee to articulate its strengths and weaknesses and, on the basis of its report, declare the need for a more effective curriculum and the conditions required to make the necessary changes? How can we change the curriculum of a college, one that has served the community admirably for several decades, without knowing why we should change the existing curriculum?"

"As far as I know, the answer to your question is no, but I have a strong feeling that the desired change is one response to the financial crisis the college is facing and that which seems to threaten the existence of the college. This crisis has become chronic during the past few years. It would help to create a new and hopefully more attractive image of the college. The board expects a balanced budget, and the president is trying to achieve this objective. A change of the curriculum helps to create this kind of image. The board wants Webster to remain the leading liberal arts institution in the state. Can it keep this image if it does not appear to the public as a progressive and innovative college, one that prepares its students for the most successful professions in the South? But from my point of view, the image they are trying to create is nothing more than a public mask."

"A mask?"

"Of course. How can the college change its curriculum if it does not also change the conditions under which it can be implemented? If the present budget is in deficit, if it cannot pay its bills or raise the salaries of its employees, how can it transform the existing teaching conditions? As we saw earlier, a college is excellent inasmuch as its teaching is excellent. The dean wants to change the curriculum without changing these conditions, which means he is seeking cosmetic, not real, change. How can you convince possible donors that the money they will donate will in fact contribute to the development of the college? Would you donate a substantial sum of your money to a poorly led or administered college, one that cannot support its faculty and academic program?"

"If the college truly aims at excellence in teaching as its emblem reads, it is more appropriate, more realistic, and more honest to perfect the existing teaching conditions, conditions that take into serious consideration the recent developments in art, science, religion, politics, and economics. Unfortunately, President Hammond and his dean want a curriculum that looks new and different. They naively apply the saying 'seeing is believing.' This is why they are changing the landscape of the college—brand-new fancy buildings, beautiful flowers, clean grounds, convenient parking lots, and so forth. They are trying to rebuild the college after the model of the corporation. Teachers are employees, students are clients, and the products the college delivers are information and professional skills, not minds cultivated in human values as well as in professional skills. Is the market interested in cultivated minds? It should be interested in them, but it is not. Is it an accident that President Hammond's priority has been to establish a graduate school of business, not a graduate school of humanities?"

"What you say seems to make good sense," Dr. Lawson interjected, "but why would Beardsley allow himself to be the handmaid of the president?"

Dr. Adams was unable to stop the burst of a chuckle through his dry throat. He took a big gulp of water and continued: "This is a complex and in fact a tricky question. But I can briefly remark that Dean Beardsley is not a real dean. He does even know how to conduct a faculty meeting! He has never been the dean of the faculty; he is an agent of the president. I doubt that his vocation in life is the promotion of liberal arts education. One member of the psychology department remarked to me that he is a 'frustrated theologian,' like most of the people he has hired for the religion department. He is simply a yes-man!"

"But he speaks well on formal occasions, and he seems to know much about education."

"This is exactly where the problem lies. He has memorized the history of liberal arts education from its inception to the recent past. He pretends to think and act as if Webster is a clone of one of the famous universities in the Northeast. Speaking well is one thing, and administering well is something else. Good administration is always a creative activity. The comical aspect of this dean is that he neither encourages nor tolerates the creative minds of his faculty. What is at issue is the possibility of a creative vision and wise leadership, both of which are absent. Beardsley administers through a network of cronies in the different departments. He 'reads' the members of the faculty and attracts those who can be used in achieving his wishes or plans smoothly—of course for a price. He always indirectly works on the assumption that every human being has a price. The faculty are human beings; therefore, each faculty member has a price. If he cannot read you because you are honorable, because you act on principle, or if you stand in his way, he tries to neutralize or marginalize you.

"But what is perverse about this dean is that he does not possess a real vision of liberal arts education at Webster. A person with such a vision is a reformer, but he is not. So far, all the changes made by him are superficial. Instead of ensuring higher standards of instruction, he let the existing standards fall; instead of hiring competent faculty, he hired mediocre faculty, either cronies or cronies of his cronies; instead of transforming the faculty into a community of scholars and learners, he distanced himself from the faculty and the students. The college is nowadays more an agglomeration than a conglomeration. Legalism is the principle of its administration, not moral or rational principle."

Dr. Lawson's eyes widened when he heard this characterization of Dean Beardsley. He had never thought that he would hear such a characterization from the lips of Dr. Adams. "But he is viewed as a competent dean," Dr. Lawson said.

"It is better to say a better politician. The difference between the two is big. Webster does not need politicians; it needs competent leaders; it needs minds on fire; it needs creative minds and lovers of humanity; and it needs reformers. A college that is academically successful will never face financial problems, but we have been in an ongoing quagmire of financial problems for many years now. On the contrary, genuine leadership will certainly attract generous donations from its graduates, friends, foundations, even from the federal government—"

But Dr. Adams could not continue the development of this point because Janice softly knocked at the door. "Lunchtime!" she said as she moved closer to the two friends.

"Time flies!" Dr. Adams said.

"Yes, it does!"

Dr. Adams's greatest aspiration as a former faculty member of Webster College was to see the college as a living, growing, and constantly developing center of learning, teaching, and research. He was unable to conceive the possibility of excellent teaching apart from research. How can the ideas you discuss with your students be drops of fire, of insight, of knowledge if those ideas do not originate from a living mind, from a mind that thinks them? And how can the mind think such ideas if they do not originate from a fresh activity of research—inquiry? The inquiring mind is a bed of intellectual fire. The fire of the ideas you discuss should be sparks that originate from that bed.

Although Dr. Adams ate his lunch with a modicum of appetite, and although he followed the instructions Dr. Hardy and Janice prescribed, he felt somewhat uneasy when he reclined in his bed and gazed into the infinity of the space that was packed in the corner of his room. But he was unable to relish the pleasure of that gaze because the sedative he had taken prompted him to sleep—against his will.

One of Dr. Lawson's students, David Brandon, was sitting in a chair next to his bed when Dr. Adams opened his eyes to the living world. For him, sleep time was a kind of prison primarily because one's consciousness during this period is bounded by the infinity of nonbeing. The world of light is the world of being, while the world of darkness is the world of nonbeing. When we sleep, we slide into the world of darkness. Dr. Adams's eyes sparkled with gladness when he saw David sitting next to his bed. He smiled and slowly stretched his hand to him. David clasped it fervently with his two hands. He loved the only living philosopher in his life. He was a physics and philosopher major, and Dr. Lawson was his advisor. He had introduced David to Dr. Lawson and had slowly established an intimate friendship with him. David had fallen in love with his philosopher. He had already visited him a few times, mainly to inquire about his well-being and ask him some difficult philosophical questions. Frankly, he desired to visit the professor more frequently than he did, but he did not, not only because he did not have time but because he was shy. David was writing his honors paper on Plato, and he had been discussing its thesis with Dr. Adams.

"I am happy to see you, David!" Dr. Adams said. David's lips trembled a little. He could not speak, not immediately; he was flustered. Who would not be flustered in the presence of a moral and intellectual monument? The fluster is perplexing specially when the person who experiences it is young and innocent. Dr. Adams noticed his confusion, with which he was familiar, and added, as if he did not notice the fluster, "Tell me, my dear, how are your classes going?"

"My classes are fine. Oh, Dr. Adams, although you have not been teaching as a regular faculty member, and although you have been teaching one seminar now and then, the college is not the same without you, sir."

"But I am not the college, David. I used to be one of its teachers."

"Not all teachers are teachers—not like you. No comparison, sir! Yes, you used to be, and to me you still are, one of its regular teachers, but your spirit, your presence, you, are everywhere. I and many of my friends see the college through you. No wonder Dr. Lawson loves you!" Like David, Dr. Adams was becoming flustered. He was unable to respond to David. He simply looked into his eyes thoughtfully.

"David—" Dr. Adams began to say, but he could not complete his sentence only because two ladies slowly, almost on tiptoe, entered the room. Jasmine and Eve walked directly toward Dr. Adams's bed. Jasmine kissed him on his right cheek and Eve on his forehead.

"Good afternoon!" Jasmine said, focusing her attention on the sick man's face.

"You and Eve bring light into my world, Jasmine!" Dr. Adams said, stretching his hand to Eve. He kissed her hand and kept it in his for a few seconds. "I want you to meet my dear student, David Brandon, one of the best students in the philosophy and physics departments. I can say that he is my prize student at the present. He is now doing research for his honors paper. It is a pleasure to be his advisor on this project."

David came to his feet and looked at the guests with a solemn, respectful expression on his face. "Jasmine is Dr. Lawson's wife; she is a teacher at Murrah High School. Eve is their daughter; she will be attending Webster College next fall, perhaps this summer," Dr. Adams said.

"I am pleased to meet you!" David said, looking at Jasmine and Eve with two timid eyes. He ran to the other side of the room and brought a chair. "Please be seated, Mrs. Lawson!" He was so embarrassed, he could not look at Jasmine and her daughter. He had never met Dr. Lawson's wife and daughter before. Seeing them for the first time was quite an experience for him. Then David moved his chair closer to Jasmine's and said with the same tone of voice, "This is for you, Eve. Please sit!" He stood at the foot of the bed and directed his eyes mainly at Dr. Adams.

"Thank you, David!" said Jasmine. "I too am pleased to meet you. It is an honor to meet Dr. Adams's prize student. No one can remain intellectually silent in the intimate company of this learned man." David's embarrassment, intermixed with a deep feeling of shyness, magnified. He was almost beside himself.

"I am just a student, Mrs. Lawson."

But Eve was not less shy and flustered than the young man who had welcomed her deferentially. She sat in the chair without looking him. She simply could not look at him! And yet she was looking at him without looking only because his presence, which emanated from the purity of his heart, not to mention his serious bent of mind, was visible to the eyes of her soul. Did she have to speak with David or even thank him for offering his chair to her? I wonder!

"How are you doing, Seneca?" Jasmine asked after she sat in her chair. "I heard that you will be spending a few days at home."

"Yes, you heard correctly, but only God knows how long I shall stay there."

"A long time, Seneca!" she said, interrupting Dr. Adams. "Stanley, Eve, and I shall come to your house, and we shall keep you company all if not most of the time. I shall cook your favorite meals. You cannot dismiss us from your home!"

"Would you allow students and friends to visit you, Dr. Adams?" David asked.

"Of course, any time. His home has always been open to friends, colleagues, even to strangers so far as I know," Jasmine remarked.

"Yes, dear Jasmine, but who wants to visit a dying man?"

"But who can resist to visit a flame of life? Such a flame does not die. It is always bright, always lovable, always attractive, always precious!"

"You are the only person in this world who knows how to disable my power of speech!"

"No, Seneca, you do not see, maybe because you refuse to see, your power of speech. People speak with their tongue, but you speak with the voice of love, of wisdom, especially of your presence. Why would these two flares of youth," she said, pointing to David and then to Eve, "come here to be with a dying man? By the way, Eve has a load of questions. As you recommended, she read Plato's *Republic*. She told me that she enjoyed it very much. She wants to discuss her questions with you. I have a feeling that she will follow in your footsteps."

"Are you sure?" Dr. Adams asked, looking at Eve.

"Yes, Uncle Seneca. I plan to read more of Plato's dialogues. I would be grateful if you prepare a reading list for me."

This warm gathering of strangers and friends was interrupted by Janice's appearance. She was carrying a box filled with small paper cups containing pills, some to be taken immediately and some during the night. She stopped in the middle of the room and looked at the guests with a feeling of pleasure. She had already met Jasmine and Eve but not David. Her eyes lingered on David for a few moments. They were gratified with what they saw. She moved closer to that small community. "I am happy to see you, Jasmine!" she said, and then, looking at Eve, continued, "and you too, dear Eve." Her eyes embraced David again. She was unable to determine whether he was related to Dr. Adams or to the Lawsons. Dr. Adams's eyes understood Janice's desire, which he respected.

"Janice," he said, "I want you to meet David, one of the outstanding students at Webster College. He is Dr. Lawson's student, and now he is my advisee." David left the foot of the bed and greeted Janice with a soft hand-shake. "I am pleased to make your acquaintance," he said and returned to his place.

"Why are you standing? People cannot visit standing!" Janice said spontaneously, left the room instantly, and returned with a wooden chair. She placed it next to Eve's and said, "Sit! Now you can visit the right way with your teacher and these two lovely ladies."

"Do not let your eyes give you the wrong impression, David," Dr. Adams remarked. "Janice is not my nurse; she is my guardian angel. No one knows this fact but the Lawsons."

Janice visited with her patient for a few minutes. She explained the function of the medications and the time they should be taken. She also promised to return in a short time.

"Tell me, David—what is the subject of your honors paper?" Jasmine asked after Janice had left. David was happy to hear that question because answering it was his only way out of the storm of the emotions that was raging in his mind. He was shy and he knew it, but he did not know that it could rattle his consciousness, especially when the radiance of a beautiful young woman who sat next to him was dancing in his mind and heart.

But this young woman was not merely beautiful; oh no, she was a living image of beauty—of grace, of elegance, of splendor. When this kind of beauty shines through youth, you can be sure to glean the divine in it. The only thing you can do in this kind of presence is tremble, not out of fear but out of awe. But David was still young, innocent, naïve. This was the first time he had stood in the radiance of this image of beauty, which was no image but a living ray of the divine; this was the first time he had been captive to it; and this was the first time he desired to be captive to it and to delight in the captivity. He did not fumble; he could not, not at that moment. In such moments, the magic of divine beauty sweeps you off your feet and splinters you into bits of perplexity, of delectable dreams, of transport. Can you blame David for welcoming Jasmine's question? But what was strange, deliciously strange, was that Eve was not aware of the power of her beauty; she was aware of the charm, indeed elegance, of David's perplexity, and she loved it because she saw him in the purity of his mind and heart. She was satisfied, happy. She did not need assurances, explanations, arguments, promises, or any kind of verbal or bodily gestures to know what was happening to David or how she felt. One may wonder why. Hadn't she seen the soul of the man through his perplexity, through the way he acted, through the love and respect Dr. Adams showed toward him?

No matter how they meet—by accident, gradual acquaintance, cunning parents or friends, dating services, or marriage brokers—two people cannot fall in love unless this kind of divine fire unites them in the bond of love. The conditions under which they meet are irrelevant. The genuine bond of love arises from and is sanctified by this fire. This kind of bond does not weaken but strengthens as time moves on. Is it an accident that no power can sunder lovers from each other when this type of bond unites them into one soul and two individuals? Is it an accident that genuine lovers elope, sometimes commit suicide, anger their parents or priest, or prefer to live in poverty rather than live apart from each other? Unlike the intellect, the romantic heart is not a mathematician; it does not calculate. It responds to the warmth of the human heart spontaneously. This warmth is its only language!

Eve was a truly beautiful woman, but she was also an intellectual woman, a prodigy, endowed with delicate imagination, an analytical and critical mind, and a refined aesthetic sense. Dr. Lawson and Jasmine were in love with each other. Eve was an objectification of this love. She grew as an individual as they grew in their love for each other. The more they grew in their love, the more this growth was reflected in the growth of their daughter. My grandmother, who used to tell me stories when I was a young boy, told me when I was about to graduate from high school that the creation of the world was an act of love and that the creation of civilization, of every one of its elements, was also an act of love. She was convinced that the power of love is the source of everything good in this world. "You are created twice, son," she said, "when you leave the womb of your mother and when you fall in love. Your true birth is your second birth. Make sure that it is created by the fire of love that burns in your heart."

Eve had been born by and from the fire that was flaming in her parents' hearts; what is more important is that she was cultivated by the same fire. Is it an accident that she was a prodigy?

"The subject of my paper," David said in response to Jasmine's question, "is Plato's allegory of the cave." Eve's eyes shimmered with interest.

Jasmine knotted a soft frown on her forehead and looked at David with curious eyes. "This is one of the most central yet most difficult metaphors in the *Republic*," Jasmine said. "Do you have a focus or a thesis?"

"I shall preface my discussion with an acknowledgement. This is not simply a formal expression of recognition; it is an expression of a feeling rooted in my consciousness. This feeling has been locked up in me for a long time. I now think that it is time for me to express it to him in his presence, and yours. It is a feeling of profound gratitude to the man who inspired not only my paper and its thesis but also the new life I am now leading. This man is not an ordinary human being. He kindled in my mind a sense of curiosity and a desire for life. I was a groper; now I have a purpose. I was blind; now I see. I was apathetic; now I care. I did not know what beauty was; now I adore it. I owe everything I am and everything I have to this man who was willing to see me privately and answer many questions I had about my life and myself."

Jasmine was smiling while David was making his confession, which he called acknowledgement. But Eve was listening to him with rapt attention. The breadth of her eyes resonated in the depth of her attention. She could not lift her eyes off David's face.

"The thesis I plan to discuss and defend is that teachers at the beginning of every course they teach should begin with an interpretation and discussion of the allegory of the cave."

"Why?" Eve, who had finished reading Plato's *Republic,* asked.

"This question darts at the substance of my defense," David said rather timidly.

"Have you developed your defense?" she asked pointedly.

"I have sketched an outline. . . . "

"Can I hear it?"

"It may strike you as naïve. . . . "

"I would like to hear it," Eve said with an anxious voice. It was obvious to her mother and to Dr. Adams that Eve's mind was on fire. Both of them knew that her enthusiasm was not haphazard and that it was causally related to her reflection on the *Republic*. They remained silent, but their silence was a silence of love.

"Let me first state," David said, "that my thesis sprang from deep reflection on the significance of the allegory of the cave in light of Plato's overall vision of the good city. I tend to think, thanks to Dr. Adams, that one of the most important values implied in this allegory is that it functions as a metaphor that reveals the central aim of education and the structure of the process of its realization. Every course the student takes should be viewed as a part of the teaching–learning activity.

"I shall begin with an analysis of the basic structure of the allegory, which consists of four worlds—the world of the dark cave, or ignorance; the world of physical reality, or opinion; the world of Ideas, or understanding; and the world of the sun, or knowledge. Second, I shall present an interpretation of these elements. Third, I shall discuss the implications of the ascent from the world of the cave to the world of the sun and emphasize that this is the task of education—to lift the mind from the world of ignorance to the world of knowledge. I here assume that the teacher should assume that the student is a resident of the first world and that her aim is to ascend to the world of knowledge. Throughout this discussion, I shall spotlight the dynamics of the learning and growing processes."

"I have a hunch, just a hunch," Eve said, "that your plan is rather ambitious. Can it be achieved in an honors paper? What do you think?"

"I agree with you. I too feel that it is ambitious. This is a main reason that I shall beg for Dr. Adams's advice, not now but during the next few days when he is in a position to answer this and other questions I have. At any rate, I hope to see him daily, primarily to inquire about his health. He is the guiding light of my life. I do not know whether I can see well without this light."

David's eyes were fixed on Jasmine's face when he made his last remark. But Dr. Adams, who understood David more than David understood himself, curled his lips inward. His sensibility could not tolerate praise. But David was young, and he felt a strong urge to express himself that way. Was it because he knew that his teacher was dying and that he, David, was unable to accept this imminent event? Was it because he was overwhelmed by a surge of warm emotions he could not control? Was it because he subconsciously desired to acknowledge the noble role Dr. Adams played in his growth as a human being? No one can answer these questions perfectly, but it seems that "yes" would be an appropriate answer to these questions.

"David . . ." Dr. Adams said, but he did not complete his sentence. He simply gaped into his student's face with solemn silence.

It was an intensely awkward moment to Dr. Adams, Jasmine, Eve, and David. Everyone understood what David had said, and everyone understood Dr. Adams's admonishing yet compassionate response to David. It was a human moment at its best. Jasmine confirmed it: "Eve and I shall be at your home tomorrow at noon. We shall bring your lunch and ours with us. I believe that Stanley will be able to join us. And you, David, plan to visit Dr. Adams—am I right?"

"Yes, Mrs. Lawson, it has been my wish to visit him daily. I only hope he does not object."

Dr. Adams smiled, and his smile was a radiant expression of approval.

FOUR

David and Eve Fall in Love

As he always did, Master Death was standing at the foot of the bed when Dr. Adams woke up on the following morning. It took him a few seconds to recognize the figure of this undesirable visitor. He was annoyed by his presence and disturbed by his pretentions. He was unable to believe that Master Death was a real being or that he was an incarnation of the reality of death because death, Dr. Adams thought, did not exist, and even if it existed, it was impossible to be transformed into human embodiment. No line of reasoning, no matter its soundness, could convince Dr. Adams of the reality of such an embodiment. Logical arguments can prove the truth or falsity of propositions, but they cannot create or destroy real objects. Again, he had never expected to meet this kind of personality. No one could! Anomalies are rare, but this one was unbelievable, yet it seemed to be believable! How could you unbelieve what you actually confront and experience with your eyes and mind?

But then, how could Dr. Adams explain the supernatural powers of Master Death? He was not only a good logician; he was also able to perform supernatural acts, e.g., appearing and disappearing at will or assuming the form of any existing object. This unsettling fact stood before Dr. Adams's mind as a challenge. He was convinced, without a shred of doubt, that supernatural phenomena, be they acts or objects, did not exist. And yet he was unable to answer this question, and he was also unable to recognize or admit to himself that he was confronting a supernatural being. Was he hallucinating? No, because the figure that was standing before him at the foot of his bed was real, and the conversations he had been having with him

91

were equally real. Indeed, they were logical and in some cases persuasive. As he had in the past, Dr. Adams decided to wait and see whether this anomalous situation would have a clear conclusion.

"Good morning, Dr. Adams!" Master Death said. "It seems to me that you still have doubts about my identity and the purpose of my visits, even when you are standing at the Edge, where your vision can dialectically move from the realm of being, which you have loved so much, and the realm of nonbeing, which awaits you. I do not need to remind you of the noble and admirable life you have lived, and I do not need to say that you will linger in the hearts and minds of many people for a long time and that you will be a living monument in the history of Webster such a history is ever written. You deserve all this honor and much more, as I affirmed earlier. However, the purpose of my visits is to convince you that I am Master Death, that I am its human embodiment, and that you will not be completely fulfilled, or complete, to borrow a word from you, unless you recognize the truth of my reality. The point I would like to bring to your attention is that you have devoted your life to the promotion of goodness in a world that is hostile to the real good." Throughout this part of his speech, Dr. Adams's eyes were focused on the visitor's icy lips. "In your lectures as well as in your books, you argued that 'death' signifies 'cessation of life or sensation'—nothing else. This proposition stands as a denial of my existence and my mission. I cannot accept it. It is never too late to do the good. Explaining and teaching the truth about my reality, even when you are dying, is never too late. What you now say or believe will reverberate in the world of the intelligentsia after your death! You cannot shrink from this obligation. You have lived as a genuine human being, but your life contradicts your teaching. It is painfully sad for you to say farewell to the world or shrink from doing the good even when you are dying. The good in this case is telling the truth. Am I correct in saying that you subscribe to Epicurus's view of the meaning and reality of death?"

This question elicited a cynical chuckle from Dr. Adams. He thought that Master Death spoke like one of his students of philosophy. He wondered whether he should indulge in this kind of conversation. But Master Death, who was reading his mind, continued. "I am serious, Dr. Adams. I mention Epicurus because, like you, he was an honorable individual and because his philosophical intuition is a good starting point for our conversation today. Moreover, one has to climb a mountain, reach its top, and then descend it if she wants to have an adequate idea of the mountain as a whole. Similarly, one has to live the totality of her life to comprehend its meaning and destiny adequately. A wise man such as you is in the best position to theorize on the meaning and reality of death."

"What proposition would function as a starting point?" Dr. Adams asked.

"The assertion that 'death' signifies cessation of life or sensation."

"This proposition is based on the assumption that we do not know what death is like before we come into being or what it will be like after we pass out of being, even when we are standing at the Edge. No one has informed us (which is impossible because we did not yet exist) that we would be born or what it would be like to be alive. Again, no one has informed us about the end of our lives or what it would be like to be dead. As far as I know, we are passing ripples in the cosmic process of whose cause or purpose we remain ignorant. Our emergence in the cosmic process and our departure from it is a mystery that no one has yes deciphered.

"Next, we cannot make any intelligible statement or make any cognitive claims about something we do not experience empirically or intellectually. The only thing we can experience and therefore judge is our life here and now on the face of this planet. This experience says that 'death,' if it has any meaning, is simply 'cessation of life or sensation.' It would be a blunder to reify something that does not exist, and it would be foolish to reify the cessation of the life of a human being. Why, then, reify the end point of the life of a human being? Therefore, your claim that you are Master Death or that you are an embodiment of a phenomenon we cannot experience is not only misleading and cognitively vacuous, but also an insult to human intelligence. I suggest that you speak and act as your true self—who are you? Let me, before you respond to my question, say that the fact you show some supernatural powers cannot be used as a compelling argument that death is real or that you are Master Death. All such demonstrations cannot convince a rational being of your claims. The only power that establishes the truth of any claim is the power of reason, not magic, not intimidation, and certainly not wizardries.

"But the more important reason," Dr. Adams added, "is that the human being is essentially a lump of flesh, of living matter; as such, it comes into being and passes out of being the way the rocks, the trees, and the flies come into and pass out of being. Do material objects such as the rock, the tree, or the fly wonder about death or its meaning? We have no right to judge whether they wonder or know what it means for them to die. Again, we do not know what will happen to us after we cease to exist; therefore, we cannot speak of death since we cannot observe it after we die."

"You seem to imply," Master Death intervened, "that when an object comes into being, continues to exist for a while, and then passes out of being, it retains its identity during its existence."

"Not at all! No matter its kind, as soon as an object comes into being, it begins to pass out of being. The individual being we are talking about is in a continual process of becoming—constantly coming into being and constantly passing out of being. It is a constantly changing object. Every existing object is a trajectory of time and in time. This assertion applies to physical and mental objects. When I say it is a process, I mean it is a unit of time; its fabric is time. Put differently, time is the stuff out of which it is made. But it also exists in the medium of time—the cosmic process. Each object, which is a quantum of time, is an integral element of cosmic or universal time. It emerges as such as a unit in the march of the cosmic process or time. What I have just said is an application of Heraclitus's dictum that we cannot step twice in the same river, not even once, because its water is constantly changing and because our leg is also constantly changing.

"It should not be strange, then, to say that existing, or living, is a continual process of existence. Every object is a series of continually changing states. The extinction of the series means the end of the series. More concretely, it signifies the incapacity of the series to undergo any further changes. For example, consider the death of a zinnia plant. It exists and continually renews itself during spring, summer, and fall. Its capacity to renew itself decreases toward the fall and fades by its end. We can observe how its leaves gradually dry and fall to the ground, and we can also observe its last leaves falling off until its death."

"But," Master Death said, interrupting Dr. Adams, "if we say that an object is changing, it would follow that it does not have permanent identity."

"Correct. The identity of any object, physical or mental, is always relative; an object is never exactly self-same. It constantly maintains some of the essential, or defining, aspects of its preceding identity—a second, a week, a month, or several years ago—that endow the object with its identity. For example, the huge oak tree that sits in the middle of my backyard is the same oak tree my father planted twenty-five years ago, yet it is completely different. I know it is the same tree, but it is not the same tree. How can we explain this seeming contradiction? Despite a continual change in several ways, despite its being different, it has retained its essence as an oak tree. Although the basic features that constitute this essence are different, nevertheless, the core that makes up this essence has lingered through the intervening years—from the moment it was born to this day. If a genetic engineer were to change the structure of this essence, it would certainly lose its oak-essence; consequently, it will not anymore be the oak tree it was. The identity of an object is never mathematically exact, complete, or absolute. It is, as I said earlier, always relative. There is no need for me now to give a physical or metaphysical explanation of the dynamics that underlie the possibility of change in nature and human life. They are based on the most recent scientific and metaphysical findings; they are descriptive in character. They are intended to shed some light on the dynamics of change as a basis of identity.

"The continual process of change is expansive and contractive in nature. Some aspects change by expanding or adding to the being or essence of the object; others change by contracting its being. Some years ago, I was a child, but now I am a shriveled old man. The child I was is quite different from the man I am now, and yet I am the same being I was as a child. My real identity has been undergoing constant—partial but continual—change, of course, gradually during the intervening years. In every change, some aspects are lost and others are gained.

"It seems to me that we should examine what people call 'death' within the context of the essential nature of reality: process or change."

"Your logic is powerful, and your analysis of change and identity is, I think, lucid. No thoughtful and critical mind should disagree with you, and any inquirer into the nature of reality would learn from you. It is not an accident that you are a luminary in the state of Mississippi. But the analysis you have just advanced is either incomplete or suffers from a serious shortcoming."

Dr. Adams suddenly raised his eyebrows with an obvious expression of astonishment. He felt an urge to know the source of Master Death's complaint. But Master Death not only noticed Dr. Adams's astonishment; he also discerned the feeling from which it emanated.

"Your analysis of process, thanks to that sage Heraclitus and to your profound understanding of the implications of his insight into the nature of reality, is formidable. The last major metaphysicians, Hegel, Bergson, and especially Whitehead, would certainly agree with you and you with them. Dr. Adams, you have failed to take into consideration an important factor. Your analysis of process seems to be confined to physical objects such as rocks, trees, and animals. But human beings are not only material objects; they are also human objects. They are not merely lumps of flesh but human lumps of flesh. They are rational beings capable of acting according to the laws of their humanity, which are different from the laws of nature, as you have frequently argued in your lectures and books. Even though their bodies function according to the laws of nature, they can act voluntarily as human beings, which means they can chart their life and live according to the chart, not according to the laws of nature but nevertheless consistently with those laws. They are not merely conscious like animals and some plants but also self-conscious. They exist and they can know what it means to exist, unlike the rest of natural objects.

"Now, Dr. Adams, do you imply in your analysis of process, which is very brief, that what you said about process in nature applies to human beings? What does it mean for a human being to exist as a process, and what does it mean for her to die? Is her death identical with the death of the rock? At one point of your discussion, and following the celebrated Epicurus, you said that 'death' signifies cessation of life or sensation. But Epicurus implied that the human being is essentially a chunk of matter. He also implied that this chunk does not change, and yet he said that it comes into and passes out of being. He reduced the human being to a material object—do you implicitly subscribe to his view of human nature? That is, the human dimension of the human being reducible to matter? If it is not, what does it mean for the human being to die?"

"I do not subscribe to Epicurus's view of human nature, but I believe that his fundamental intuition of death is, as I discussed earlier, both sound and realistic: death is the cessation of life or sensation. The moment of cessation is an absolute end. But the real question is, what does it mean for the human being to die, assuming that he is a chunk of matter? The difference between the death of the tree or the rock is subjective in character. Unlike human beings, plants and rocks lack subjectivity. Human beings can know that all things die and that they too will die. This is why many contemporary philosophers have focused their attention on the meaning of death. It seems to me that an answer to this question should begin with an analysis of the Heraclitean dictum, which I tried to elucidate a few minutes ago, namely, process is the essence of all reality, natural and human."

"But," Master Death asked, interrupting Dr. Adams, "is the human dimension of human beings a process?"

"You cannot speak of a human element apart from the human being as an organic unity of body and humanity. The human being as a whole is a process, a continual process of change; therefore, the human dimension is a process, the same process that constitutes the reality of the human as an individual."

"But what is the ontic status of the human dimension of the human being?"

"There is no reason for me to raise the classical 'mind–body' question that has plagued philosophical discourse during the past twenty-five centuries. But if I take the most recent findings in science, which no sane philosopher can reject, on the nature of the human dimension, I can say that the human element is an essential element of the body of any member of the human species. This element emerged in the course of time. Its emergence contradistinguishes this species from the rest of animal species. Its life and death are intertwined with the life and death of the body because its being is intertwined with the being of the body. It is centered in the brain and performs the function usually attributed to human beings—thinking, feeling, willing, and creating. Consciousness and self-consciousness are the primal source of these four capacities

"Now we can address more directly your basic concern: what does it mean to die as a human being? A natural object such a rock passes out of being without consciousness or knowledge of its identity. But the human being is conscious of and knows its identity. It also knows what it means to exist and live as a human being, but more importantly, it knows, or should know, that its identity is a process, which means that its existence consists of an ongoing transition from one state of being into another state. That is, she knows that the being she was a moment ago—an hour, a week, a month, or years ago—does not exist. But if this process of transition is essentially a continual process of coming into being of continually succeeding states of being, which makes up the life of the human being, it should follow that the life of the human being is a continual process of living and dying; put differently, *it is a continual process of living death.* I make this assertion, which is a conclusion of my preceding discussion, because we as human beings can experience the passage of every new and receding state of our being. We have this kind of experience when we are in a state of anxious waiting. Don't we experience the presence of the preceding moment in the succeeding or present moment? How often do we recall the preceding moment and regret or delight in it? Can we experience this regret or delight if the preceding moment is not present in the present moment, if it does not linger, at least for a while—albeit partially since nothing recurs? This assertion is based on the Heraclitean insight that we cannot experience—anything—twice; therefore, our memory of an experience is never the same.

"We know what it means for the preceding moment to be a past moment only because we experience its passing. We can experience this passing because we witness, or live, it in the succeeding state of our being; that is, we experience the emergence of this state from the preceding state that has just passed away. The basis of this experience is the fact of its partial continuation into the succeeding states of being. In other words, we know, at least at the level of intuition, what it means for our being to be a process of continual coming into being, which is a continual process of living and dying.

"This realization is the basis of our answer to the question, what does it mean to die as a human being? *To know what it means to die as a human being is to know what it means to live as a human being!*"

"Your line of reasoning is provocative, and I am provoked by the way you have arrived at the conclusion that human life is a living death. But first, if human life is living death, don't you acknowledge the reality of death, therefore my own reality that you have so far denied? Second, if human life is living death, what does it mean to die when one reaches the Edge, where you are now standing with one foot in the realm of being and the other in the realm of nonbeing? Shouldn't we make a distinction between human death and the mere cessation of the life of the human being? Doesn't the question, What does it mean to die as a human being? lose its significance, if not its meaning, if death is reduced to mere passing way? For if I know that my extinction is an ongoing process and that my life is a shadow that hovers over this process, shouldn't I ask, what is the point of striving for any type of human ideal?

"Should the answer to our question, what does it mean to die as a human being? be answered with, There is no point to strive for any ideal because what seems to be a process of life is in fact a process of death? But Dr. Adams, I do not expect an answer from you this morning only because I hear footsteps approaching your door. Your life is short. It is, I think, wise to enjoy the company of your friends, especially the company of the young man who will enter the room momentarily," Master Death said with a malignant wink in his right eye and then added, "Don't you think that my visits to you should at least be an indication that I am real?" He threw a serious look at Dr. Adams and vanished.

It was Sunday. To Dr. Adams's pleasant surprise, the footsteps he heard were David's. Dr. Adams welcomed him with a cheerful "Good morning!" Dr. Adams initiated the greeting only because he knew that David was shy and so he might be agitated. He was right because David walked timorously when he approached his advisor's bed. Bright young people are frequently intimidated by highly respected, competent, and erudite teachers. They fear them, and they love them. They love them because they know, because they are creators, because they are honest, because they are lovers, and they fear them because they are monuments standing on pedestals. They aspire to be such monuments, but can they be such monuments? Can they plunge into the ocean of the human mind?

"How was your week?" Dr. Adams asked.

"It was a good week, sir, but with one exception—"

"An exception?" Dr. Adams wondered with a fatherly smile. "What is it?"

"A feeling of guilt was boiling in my mind when I left you yesterday."

"Why?"

"My answer to Eve's question yesterday was rather foolish, in fact embarrassing. I felt guilty. This feeling has not left me. The plan of my honors paper is really ambitious; Eve was right. I have been thinking about it. I need your help in articulating my thesis."

"The help should come from you; if it does not come from your mind, you can neither explain it nor defend it. Moreover, if it does not come from your mind, you cannot say that the paper is yours. If I am to render any help, it would be formal. I can give an opinion on the significance or basis of the thesis and the viability of the method you choose to defend it." David fixed a thoughtful look at Dr. Adams for a few seconds. The look was accompanied with two pursed lips. "If I were you, David," Dr. Adams continued, "I would reflect on the meaning of the allegory: Why did Plato construct it? What is its purpose? What are its basic elements? What does each part mean or represent? Finally, under what conditions can it serve as a model of education? Imagine yourself as a prisoner in that dark cave. Imagine how this darkness creates an itch in your mind to escape from the cave all the way until the moment your eyes are enamored not only by sunlight but especially by the sun itself. Yes, analyze and then evaluate every major experience you undergo in your ascent from the cave to the sun with the following question in mind: how does this journey serve in shedding light on the possibility of education as a process of growing intellectually and affectively?

"You do not need to examine every element and every aspect of your understanding of the allegory. Select one aspect and explore it critically. Make sure that you have a purpose and a method of achieving the purpose."

"I comprehend the fundamental structure of the allegory—" David started to say, but he could not complete his sentence only because he heard the wheels of a small cart rolling toward his teacher's room; but the teacher did not, for a reason David could not decipher, see a reason to stop speaking. He also had something on his mind. He took advantage of this momentary lull and made the following remark:

"David," Dr. Adams said affectionately, "do not lose Eve!" He made this remark with a concerted effort, as if it were his last chance to make it. He paused for a second and tried to breathe but could not. It seemed to David that the air Dr. Adams was trying to inhale was stuck in his throat, as though two hostile hands were trying to suffocate him. He promptly rose to his feet, looked at Dr. Adams's face, which was frighteningly pale, and then turned his own face toward the advancing cart. It was covered with an assortment of medications. Janice was behind it. One glance at the frantic David and then at Dr. Adams, who was struggling for breath, was enough to arouse a feeling of alarm in her mind and heart. She left the cart in the middle of the room and ran toward her beloved patient. His eyes were closed, his face was ashen, and his chest was heaving slowly, very slowly. She sprinted to the nurses' station and returned with an oxygen apparatus. She placed it next to Dr. Adams's bed, inserted a plastic tube in his nostrils, and turned on the apparatus. A few seconds later, Dr. Adams looked at his guardian angel. A beam of love, of appreciation, of gratitude flew from his eyes into hers. She bent over his body and kissed him on the forehead. No words were exchanged between them. There was no need for words. When the heart speaks, the lips remain silent.

Baffled but more scared, more unsettled than baffled, for he had never witnessed such a spectacle before, David was staring at the nurse with utter amazement, not the kind we usually feel when we witness something strange, dramatic, even spectacular, but something we feel in the presence of the miraculous. But the miracle David witnessed was not a transgression of a law of nature, even logic—no, not at all; it was an epiphanic event, an event that revealed to him the true mystery of human love, of the love that originates from the spark that gives rise to our humanity. He was mesmerized, and he was elated. He had read about this kind of love in the books of the poets, the saints, and the mystics, but he had never dreamed to see it as a shining presence in his personal experience, especially of his dear teacher. Was it another lesson he had learned from him?

Even if Dr. Adams had desired to give his prize student a lesson in the art of human loving, he could not have either intended or planned it at that moment. The way he acted and lived, and now the way he was struggling with the question of the meaning of human life, was in itself an event that enhanced his understanding of a fundamental truth of human existence. We may hide this truth under the rug of our life, we may belittle it, and we may fight it, but we cannot ignore it when we stand at the Edge. We can teach people by lectures, books, movies, conversation, and sermons, but one of the most important means of teaching is by experience, by watching how wise people make decisions, act, and live. There are no ready-made prescriptions or rules for how we should face the difficult problems we face in the course of our individual lives. All the rules, prescriptions, or advice we may have ready at hand are useful indicators or recommendations for possible judgments but are never the source of such judgments because the problems and situations in which they come into being are always in the future, always new. However, some of the significant and vital problems or questions we now face frequently reveal the essence, the core, the heart of the logic of any problem or question we face as human beings. Knowledge of this essence, core, or heart is one of the most valuable gems of understanding we receive from people of practical wisdom.

Although he was young and naïve, although his mind was still a rich possibility of learning and growing, and although he was not yet articulate in the art of communication, David was a perceptive, discriminating young man. He knew that his teacher was nearing his end, but he did not know that the end was imminent. He felt a strong desire to remain close to him, to be attentive to his needs if he were needed, and to give what he could give—himself. Whether this determination was shaped by the spectacle he had witnessed a little while ago or whether it existed in his mind as a latent possibility, for he was so far as we know a decent person, does not matter. What matters is that he reached this determination. However, he was not the intrusive or parasitic kind of human being. He was quiet by nature and decided to stay around his teacher quietly.

Janice brought a chair and sat next to the bed facing Dr. Adams. She wanted to make sure that he was breathing normally and that he was comfortable. That was her duty as a nurse, but her desire to remain close to him originated from a caring heart. It may seem strange to some people that Janice chose to be a nurse not because she needed money, only money, although she needed money to survive, but because she had a nursing heart, because she was a healer. Nursing was her vocation in life. In fact, all her patients loved her, and all her colleagues respected her unwavering commitment to the well-being of her patients. She exchanged a few smiles with David but did not initiate a conversation with him only because all her attention was devoted to her patient. How could she talk about this or that subject, no matter how interesting or important it might be, if she was sitting next to a patient she loved and especially if that patient was standing on the Edge? Usually visitors, especially family members, create much meaningless talk, and in some cases noise, in this kind of situation, which only reveals an orientation of selfishness and indifference to the patient. Janice was quite aware of such visitors. For her, the sanctity of the human being could not be violated. It should always be respected. She always stood in awe before the humanity of her patients. We frequently see people as they really are in times of trouble and in times of sickness. The human shines through the fog and the rain of such trouble or sickness!

"How do you feel, my dear?" she said when she was certain that her patient was able to communicate. She left her chair and held his right hand. As he always did, Dr. Adams lifted her hand and kissed it. A tear rolled down his cheek and landed on her hand. She wiped it with her hand and smiled. He swallowed his saliva and tried to speak but could not. He smiled. This smile was the only expression he could communicate at that moment. He turned his face toward his prize student and embraced him with a similar smile. His smiles oozed love and gratitude. "Dr. Hardy should be here any minute now," she said. "How about some juice or milk?" But Janice did not have to fetch either because the wheels of the lunch lady's rack were already reverberating through the hall. Anyway, Janice left her chair, went to the rack, and brought a tray for Dr. Adams. "You can have some juice, I think," she said. He nodded. His throat, in fact his whole body, was dry.

"Have you met David?" Dr. Adams asked with a faint voice.

"I have, but not formally." David's face was a shining image of concern. Janice saw it and felt it.

"He is a philosophy major and plans to graduate next year. He is dear to my heart!"

Janice's eyes dwelled on David's face for a few seconds. This remark produced a blush on David's cheeks. Janice noticed the blush. Sometimes the way we act and respond to the different situations we encounter in the course of our daily lives reveals much about how we truly feel and think more adequately than any type of ordinary speech. Janice felt a special liking for David, and she felt at home in his presence.

"Have you had your breakfast, David?" she asked. He felt embarrassed by the question, and his embarrassment showed on his ruddy cheeks. He was confused only because the question was unexpected, but Dr. Adams was not surprised. He knew Janice, and he knew why she had asked that question. He also knew the cause of David's embarrassment. He intervened.

"I have a hunch that he did not," Dr. Adams said, addressing Janice.

Janice dashed into the hall for a few seconds and returned with a tray. She placed it on the nightstand near Dr. Adams's bed and said, "You can place the tray on your thighs if you feel more comfortable that way. Do not be shy!"

David followed Janice's recommendation. "And you? Did you have your breakfast?" David asked.

"I did, David. Bon appétit!" she said and then turned her attention to her patient. She lifted the cover off the main plate on Dr. Adams's tray and began feeding him. She fed him in silence, and he ate in silence. Now it was Dr. Adams's turn to feel embarrassed, primarily because she fed him the way a mother usually feeds her child—with patience and a dash of care! He felt her loving heart with every morsel she placed in his mouth. We may feel powerful, we may feel independent and self-sufficient, we may feel that we sit on top of the world, and we may wear the most magnificent crown on our head, but no matter how great or powerful we are, I doubt that our greatness or power can equal the greatness and power of the love that emanates from the human heart. This kind of love is life-giving; it is a source of the creative act that gives birth to our humanity, to the spirit that energizes human progress in science, art, philosophy, and political life. But more importantly, it is the source of the inner harmony and contentment we crave as human beings. Dr. Adams understood this fact perfectly. He accepted the love he had been receiving from Janice and his dear friends. We frequently hear that we should give love and receive it gracefully, but the question I do not frequently hear is, How? What does it mean to give and receive love gracefully, and how can this dying man give or receive gracefully? But, alas, why should the question be raised if the true act of love is freely given and received?

Dr. Adams was reflecting on this aspect of human love when he was being enfolded by its warmth. The question that piqued his interest, desire, and curiosity was how to give this special human being, whose hand was the hand of love, gracefully. In general, "grace" denotes qualities such as beauty, elegance, loveliness; but this is not the kind of meaning he was pondering, even though he knew that the act of love is beautiful, elegant, and lovely. His mind was focused on the source and nature of love. The source of love, he thought, must be an inexhaustible source of giving. Giving is its essential feature. A well that does not give water is not a well; it is an empty hole. Its essence consists of giving water. Does it worry, or even think, about who receives its water? Does it ask for a reward or price for the water it gives? Does it ask how many trees or tomato plants drink from its water? The loving heart is this kind of well; it is an overflowing stream of giving. But shouldn't the plant or the human being who drinks from it be thankful for receiving water from it? Of course, yes, but exactly the way it receives it—freely. Does the human being need to express this recognition? Yes, but not to the source that gives the water. If we receive love gracefully, then we should keep it as a sacred trust in our minds and hearts truthfully, and we keep it in our minds and hearts truthfully inasmuch as we grow in giving to others freely, gracefully. The person who receives love is a witness to the act she receives.

I here assume that love is a powerful, transformative act. The essence of this transformation is growth in the power of giving. Accordingly, we receive gracefully when we cultivate the gift of love we receive and promote its fruits in the lives of others. I am not unaware of the widespread fact that, unfortunately, acts of love are commodified and that genuine lovers are frequently hurt, belittled, misunderstood, and used selfishly, nor am I unaware that the heart of many human beings is petrified. But I am convinced that the loving heart is always true to itself, always indifferent to the selfishness and hypocrisy of people, always living from its core. Could it be that the language of silence Dr. Adams and Janice spoke was the language of true love? Could it be that the young David was a novice in this kind of love?

Janice gave Dr. Adams his medications, one of which was a potent sedative and the other a painkiller. His body was getting weaker and weaker;

he knew it, and yet his mind was an overflowing stream of thought—of reflection, of analysis, of reasoning. He was responsive to anyone who engaged him in a serious conversation. He desired to talk with David about his honors paper but specially about his personal life because he knew that, although the student was a flare of intelligence and although he was morally strong, he was still pure and naïve. People like him are easy targets of hypocrites, frauds, and scoundrels. He was not a fighter; he was a peace lover. He acted on the basis of rational judgment and moral sense, not on the basis of impulse, cunning, or self-indulgence. Dr. Adams's immediate inclination when Janice left was to explain some basic aspects of existential life, but he could not only because he dozed off against his will.

David was sitting when Dr. Lawson, Jasmine, and Eve entered the room on tiptoe. Apparently, they had met Janice at the nurses' station before going into Dr. Adams's room. She must have given them a report about her patient's condition because their faces were grave when they greeted David, who stood up the instant they came in. They brought a big parcel containing lunch for everyone, including David, not knowing that Dr. Adams had had a relapse. David brought chairs from the adjoining room for Jasmine and Eve. Eve and Jasmine sat at the front end of the bed and David and Dr. Lawson at its foot. "We know what happened," Dr. Lawson said to David. "The doctor will be here in a few minutes."

No one in this gathering had a will to speak. The pleasure that had highlighted their spirits a little while ago was now changed into a grim feeling of sadness. When sadness fills the human soul, it deprives it of the power of speech, and when the sadness is sadness unto the impending death of a dear, beloved human being, it paralyzes the power of expression. Dr. Lawson was restless. He could not sit, and he could not stand either. He walked toward his friend's peaceful face and embraced it with a warm look, one that lingered for several seconds as if he were trying to tease out some secret out of it. Unconsciously, he placed his hand on Dr. Adams's shoulder and stroked it gently. His eyes never left his friend's face. It seemed to Jasmine that her husband was subconsciously bidding goodbye to his friend. This might have been one of the last occasions when he could express the deep love they shared as friends. Jasmine contemplated that scene with a deep feeling of compassion. Yes, compassion! How could that feeling have warmed up her heart had she not lived the meaning of true love with her husband?

But Dr. Lawson's gentle stroke was no ordinary stroke! It was a stroke of love, the same love that united them in the bond of friendship. It must have found its way to the dying man's consciousness, for Dr. Adams slowly opened his eyes a few seconds later. Their eyes met, and a smile danced on Dr. Lawson's lips. His smile was met by a similar smile from the lips of his friend. Jasmine, followed by Eve and David, immediately stood next to Dr. Lawson. She lowered her head and kissed Dr. Adams on the forehead. Eve kissed him on the cheek. David watched this scene with amazed eyes. He desired to express his love to his dear teacher, to acknowledge his gratitude to him, and to assure him that the time he spent with him was not in vain, but he could not. He could not speak. His mind was crowded with powerful emotions. Those emotions overpowered his power of speech. But alas, did he have to speak? He simply stood next to Eve and watched that extraordinary scene. He was an active participant nevertheless—silently.

Eve, who was also silent, suddenly stole a glance at the young man standing next to her. Tears were glittering in his eyes. He tried to hide them from her by slightly turning his face away from her, but he could not. He was shy, yes, and his shyness showed. She felt with him and for him. Like laughing, sometimes tears are infective. They were infective on that occasion. She faced him and stared into his eyes for a few long seconds; she could not withdraw her eyes from their innocent, magical, inviting depth. Sadness is usually a feeling or a mental state of sorrow, grief, or dejection. But that mystical encounter, that sadness that filled their minds and hearts, was transformed into a silent dialogue, into a conversation that transcended any mode of articulate communication, *into a communion*. This kind of experience usually takes place only when two people stand before each other *au naturel*, when they see each other for what they are in the truth of their being. What they see is lovely, captivating. Those two human young souls were captive in each other's hearts. It may seem strange, and sometimes mysterious, that the human heart can conduct this kind of conversation in moments of grief, tragedy, or disaster. But goodness, can it close its eyes before the truth of true human encounter? Can it prevent itself from embracing the truth it discerns? The truthful heart is always truthful! But again, is it strange for love to speak in sad moments? I wonder!

This burst of love in Dr. Adams's room that morning was interrupted by the entrance of Janice and Dr. Hardy. Jasmine, David, and Eve immediately moved to the foot of the bed. Dr. Adams introduced Jasmine, Eve, and

David to Dr. Hardy. "Thank you!" Dr. Hardy said after he exchanged some pleasantries with the guests.

"I have come to see you, only to see you!" Janice, who never left the doctor's side, understood the meaning of that unusual way of greeting her patient. She knew that neither he nor anyone could either stop or slow the gradual deterioration of Dr. Adams's lungs. Dr. Adams chose to leave the world the natural way, the stoic way; he also knew that the doctor's visit was a human visit. On the other hand, Dr. Adams knew that his student's ability to help him was limited, if not nil, and he also knew that he had come to see him because he loved him.

"It is good, very good, indeed, to see you, James."

Dr. Hardy did not respond to his teacher's repression of love and recognition. He simply could not!

"You will be in my heart as a source of hope, of inspiration, and of love of life. You have been one of the most precious, if not the most precious gift I have received; but I did not receive it from you, not directly. I received it from God. I am convinced that you have been his shining presence in the state of Mississippi." Dr. Hardy raised his teacher's hand and kissed it. On his way out of the room, he said to Janice, "Tend to him."

Dr. Adams's eyes, which followed his student until he vanished into the hall, did not change their position. They kept gaping into the vacant doorway for a few moments. Human presence, unlike any other type of presence, does not instantly depart; it lingers. To Dr. Lawson, Eve, Jasmine, and David, that encounter was miraculous, and Dr. Adams was its maker.

Dr. Adams's royal visitors brought their chairs close to the bed and sat in a semicircle. Dr. Adams welcomed this move with a deep sense of satisfaction. "How was the faculty meeting yesterday, Stanley?"

"Why don't we eat our lunch first?" Jasmine suggested. "I know you have much to talk about. Eve and I need to do some shopping for the kitchen. Please do not eat hospital food, Seneca. We shall prepare your supper, and we plan to cook your favorite dish—chicken spaghetti. We shall return as soon as possible."

Dr. Adams nodded; so did Dr. Lawson.

The lunch they ate was delicious. The event felt like a picnic at the River Bend.

"Please, David, join us. A shopping spree followed by a cooking party will be a good experience for you," Jasmine said after they ate their lunch. David did not expect the invitation, and he did not know how to respond to it. His primary and only purpose for being in that room was to be with his teacher. At first, he felt that it might be wrong to leave Dr. Adams for a shopping spree or a cooking party. He looked at Jasmine with embarrassed eyes as if to say, *It might be wrong to leave my teacher.* Jasmine understood the meaning of that look. "Seneca would not object!" she remarked. However, David hesitated.

"I agree with Jasmine," Dr. Adams intervened. "It would be good to join them, David. Besides, you need to discuss the thesis of your paper with Eve. Moreover, Eve would be interested in your opinion of Plato's concept of justice in the good society. How does this concept function as a basis of government? Is it a viable basis of a progressive society?"

Involuntarily, David's eyes moved from the face of his teacher to Eve's face. It was clear to him that her eyes were yearning for his company. This look was all he needed to make his decision. But did he make his decision? Did Dr. Adams facilitate the decision-making process? No, not really. The magic of those eyes and the yearning of his heart were the basis of that decision. Can reason overpower the desire of the yearning heart? When the eyes see clearly and truthfully, when the heart yearns truly, and when true yearning streams between the two loving hearts, reason does not remain silent; it blesses it. Eve kissed Dr. Adams and her father on the cheek before leaving the room. She was happy!

But before going to Kroger, Jasmine suggested a short visit to Sweeney for an ice cream cone. This suggestion was met with unanimous approval. That visit was an appropriate occasion for Jasmine and her daughter to become acquainted with David. Jasmine inquired about his personal interests, why he had chosen philosophy as a major, and whether he had friends, and she inquired about his family. She was surprised, in fact pleased, to know that his father was a doctor and his mother a nurse, but she was more pleased to discover that his father treated poor patients free of charge. But she was thrilled to discover that the reason for this practice was Dr. Brandon's firm belief that medicine was a human service, not a business. He could not understand how caring for the life of a human being could be a means for amassing money. The value of human life, he thought, could not be measured with money. The only measure for evaluating it was promotion of goodness. Medical practice could be an occasion for a satisfying, fulfilling, happy living but not for amassing wealth. "I have a feeling, David," Jasmine remarked, "that your parents are philosophical practitioners."

"Yes, they are. Both of them were philosophy majors at Baylor University. They met in their junior year. My father decided to go to medical school and my mother to nursing school. They got married shortly after they graduated from Baylor. They are still in love. They behave now the way they did when they were at Baylor! They cannot live without each other—not for one day. It sometimes feels that they were united by a mysterious bond. Oh, how I love them! I see myself in their love. I am their only child. My father did his residency in internal medicine here in Jackson at The School of Medicine. He was able to establish a clinic when he completed his residency. This is why I am at Webster. I fell in love with Dr. Adams. He reminds me of my parents."

"Do you disagree with them?"

"Oh yes, especially with my father. We frequently discuss the political problems of the day and sometimes in general. But our disagreements have been intellectual. It may seem strange to confess that I sometimes discover that he was right and I was wrong. He taught me that disagreement should be an occasion for deeper understanding, for learning. But when it comes to practical matters, I always respect their advice. They are not imperious. They respect my feelings and my privacy."

"You strike me as a serious young man, David," Jasmine remarked. "How do you spend your free time? Do you have free time? Do you have hobbies?"

David smiled. "Definitely! I love art in general but literature and music in particular. These two arts speak directly to my soul. I feel that literature is musical, and music is depictive."

"How?"

"Music does not depict the way painting does. It depicts by revealing the fullness of certain emotions, moods, and reflective states of mind. You do not see the musical image with your ordinary eyes; you see it as pure essence, as a kind of radiance. The texture of this image is not lines and colors or any kind of form but light in its infinite dimension. The world of the musical work is a world of light—"

"And literature?" Jasmine interrupted David. "In what sense is it musical?"

"Whether it is poetic, dramatic, or depictive, the stuff of the literary work is mind. I believe that the only language the mind speaks is the language of light. When you penetrate the world of the literary work, you leave the ordinary world gradually and move into a world of light. But"—David paused for a moment and added, "in addition to art, I enjoy beauty in nature and specially in human beings. Human beauty is the dwelling place of the divine."

"Are you real, David?"

"Yes, Mrs. Lawson—" David suddenly stopped and pierced a look into Jasmine's face, as if to wonder whether she was serious.

"I was joking! You should not mind my teasing you once in a while—fine?"

"Oh no!"

Poor David did not know the depth and width of his naïveté, and he did not know that, so far, he had been living as a philosophy monk, not as an ordinary young man. But again, he was still young and had a long way to go before he learned the true way of human living. He had discovered the world of the mind, and he delighted in it its splendor, its idealism, and its grandeur thanks to Dr. Adams. But he had yet to learn that human beings cannot live without bread. You cannot live by bread alone, but you cannot live without it either. People are parts of nature, and they are tethered to the society in which they live. Society is where his parents lived, and this is where he would live! The world of the mind is the light that should illuminate the world.

But what impressed Jasmine was David's purity of mind and heart, his honesty, his love of truth and beauty, and most of all his passion for life, for creation. Jasmine was a perceptive woman. She saw that David was a bundle of human potential.

During this exchange between Jasmine and David, Eve, who sat in the booth next to her mother facing the young man she admired, was listening attentively to every word he said and every gesture he made. I say "gesture" because David tended to express himself more by means of his eyes, which were always searching for the best way to express himself; his forehead, which revealed the intensity of his train of thought; and his hands, which were instruments of the ideas he was trying to communicate; than by his lips. Although he did not see himself when he was speaking, he expressed himself the way Dr. Adams did. Eve was unquestionably enamored of his soul, which revealed itself luminously during that conversation with her mother.

Later, Jasmine did not allow the young people to help her when she was preparing the spaghetti. "It is not hard to prepare this dish," she said.

"Why don't you rest a little in the living room and discuss your Plato questions? I shall be with you shortly."

Although this proposal was a most welcome opportunity for Eve and David to be alone, to feel each other's presence, in fact they were at a loss when they found themselves in the living room—he sitting on the sofa and she on a chair facing him. They stared at each other in silence for a few seconds. During those seconds, which seemed like an eternity to them, their lips trembled a little, and their hearts beat fast a little. The worlds that spread vastly in their minds were waiting to open up and reveal themselves to each other and to pour themselves into each other's worlds. This is how they felt. Where was the goddess of love? Well, she must have been attending to the needs of would-be lovers. But again, should they have waited for this all-wise and compassionate goddess? The difficulty of these two would-be lovers was not the inability to speak; it was a question of being, of moving from one heart to the other heart, of being and embracing each other's hearts, of feeling the fire that was crackling in those hearts and sizzling in them.

Both of them uttered one word simultaneously—"I." The two utterances, the two "I"s, met in the middle of the space that separated them from each other. Alas, they smiled. Their smiles were hearty—warm, delicious, mesmerizing. "Oh, Eve!" David said. But Eve did not respond to him, not verbally. She left her chair, moved to the sofa, and sat close to him. She felt the warmth of his bodily and spiritual presence intimately. He was on fire. He too felt the fire that was flaming next to him—in him, in her. They looked into each other's eyes. Those eyes were locked in the most beautiful conversation any mind could imagine or hope for. This conversation was sealed with the most tantalizing kiss.

That kiss was not a kiss, not in the ordinary sense of the word. Oh no, not in such a moment, not in that moment. That kiss was a bond. Its roots were two minds and two hearts. Frankly, no artist can describe the mystery of that bond. How can you describe a bond made of fire and consecrated by the human heart?

The two lovers sat in the warmth of their silence for several minutes. It felt as if they were in the middle of a storm and they had to wait for it to abate. During those minutes, which seemed quite a long time, they let their eyes commune with each other. It may seem strange that two pure, willing, and lucid eyes could penetrate the boundary of the world of sense and transform the sense of time, the sense of being, from its finite to its infinite mode. *A true moment of love is always an eternal now.* This eternity was shattered between Eve and David that afternoon.

"It is awfully quiet in that room, my dear!"

The two lovers smiled, also in silence. That silence was sacred!

"No, Mother, it is not quiet. We are just fine! David and I are famished."

"We should be on our way to the hospital shortly."

"I need to go home for a few minutes," David said to Eve. "I need to take a short bath and change my clothes. Besides, I have not seen my parents for two days now. They must be missing me."

"I too shall miss you!" This response sent shivers into every fiber of David's being. He took her hand and kissed it warmly. She delighted in that kiss, and her delight was intense. That was not a social or traditional kiss, and it was not a kiss of thankfulness. It was a gesture in which David sent a waft of the love that was dancing in his soul into Eve's.

The two lovers went to the kitchen together, not hand in hand but heart in heart. Their love was so dear, so sacred, they could not reveal it to the world. But again, does it matter whether the world knew or did not know about it?

"Mrs. Lawson," David said as she was drying her wet hands, "I must leave you for a little while—"

"Leave us?" Jasmine asked, interrupting the young man. "Why?"

"I have been away from home for about two days. My parents must be anxious. They want to know about Dr. Adams's condition. It is also time for me to bathe and change my clothes."

"I understand! We shall wait for you. I know that Dr. Adams would not eat his supper without you—"

"Me too!" Eve whispered spontaneously and stared into David's eyes.

Jasmine heard the whisper, but she heard much more than a whisper. She not only heard what her daughter had said; she also felt the feeling that had given rise to the whisper. She glanced at Eve's face. It was an image of human radiance. Jasmine understood what she had heard and what her daughter felt. But that glance was succeeded by another glance at David's face. It was glowing with the same radiance. He was embarrassed, as if a surge of delicious guilt had grasped his consciousness. Jasmine smiled; then she moved closer to him and kissed him on the face. Wow! It was on fire. David was on fire. A powerful drop of joy exploded in her heart. Her only way of veiling the sparks that were flying from that explosion was to say to David that he did not need a bath. But goodness, how could a body sizzling in that heat need a bath? What germs or any kind of microscopic organisms could thrive in that heat?

"Oh no, Mrs. Lawson, I should take a bath and change my clothes. I shall join you at the hospital shortly."

"Yes, my dear, you should."

But when David returned to the hospital, neither Dr. Adams nor the Lawsons were there. The room was empty, and the emptiness was dreadful. His immediate impulse was to rush to Janice's office at the nurses' station. But the whole station was empty. David stood at the counter and looked around with agitated mind and heart. Fortunately, a nurse was passing through the intersecting hall. "Please, I need help!" he asked.

"How can I help you?"

"Dr. Adams's room is empty," he said, pointing to the corridor that included Dr. Adams's room, "and the whole wing is empty."

"Oh yes, the old man had a setback. He is in a critical condition—"

"Where is he now?" David asked with anxious mind, interrupting the nurse.

"I would think he is in the intensive care unit." The floor was striped with four colored lines. "Follow the red line. It should lead you to the intensive care unit."

"Thank you so much!" He ran through a few corridors.

The door to the intensive care unit was closed but not locked. David felt a strong urge to open it slightly and take a peek. It was a rather large hall studded with rows of beds surrounded by medical machines. He scrutinized them but was unable to identify Dr. Adams' bed. A feeling of anxiety swept through his mind. He desired to see his teacher before he died. He closed the door and decided to return to the room in the hope of meeting Janice or someone from the nurses' station. But he did not have to walk far because he heard footsteps speeding behind him. He stopped and looked. Jasmine, who was returning from a visit to the restroom, was the author of the footsteps. He rushed toward her. She embraced him and led him to a guest room near the intensive care unit. Dr. Lawson and Eve were seated on a sofa, and two men were sitting on chairs next to the sofa. The two men were Webster faculty members. David sat on a chair close to Eve, and Jasmine sat next to her husband. The group were talking about Dr. Adams's condition. Dr. Lawson introduced David to the faculty members as Dr. Berry of the chemistry department and Dr. Gregory of the political science department. Dr. Lawson briefly informed the faculty members of David's identity and relation to Dr. Adams.

Eve told David that Dr. Adams had had a critical heart attack and that Dr. Hardy was attending to him. "Dr. Hardy thinks that he will not live for a long time. His lungs are very weak, and his heart is even weaker. He will be dependent on oxygen treatment until the moment of his death."

"And now?" David asked in a hardly audible voice.

"The head nurse in this unit will decide whether he can be moved to his room now or a little later. She is watching him the way a mother watches her sick child. She has been giving us reports about his progress every few minutes."

Jasmine acted as a hostess during that visit. She must have served Dr. Gregory, Dr. Berry, and her husband portions of the spaghetti she had prepared for Dr. Adams and her family. She pulled out a bowl of spaghetti and said to David, "You must be hungry. Enjoy it!"

"Thank you, Mrs. Lawson."

Eve left her seat, went to the refreshment center, returned with a bottle of water, and placed it next to his chair.

"How are your parents?" Jasmine asked David in a soft voice.

"They are doing well. They are concerned about Dr. Adams. My father said he wished he could help, but there is no need for his help only because Dr. Adams is in good hands. Dr. Hardy is the most competent doctor at The School of Medicine. However, I informed him that Dr. Adams's case was hopeless. He and my mother insisted that I stay close to him to the very end."

"We understand, son. A man such as Seneca should never be left alone."

"I wonder whether I shall ever leave him."

"How can you? He will stay with you for a long, long time!"

The love and respect that had begun to grow in Jasmine's heart for this young man grew deeper in depth. She felt an overwhelming desire to have him as a son, not merely because she did not have one and not merely because he would be an appropriate presence in her daughter's life, but especially because he was a good human being. We usually desire the company of good human beings no matter their age, profession, economic position, or social status. By its essence, goodness is attractive. Please notice how you feel, how your heart wells up with warm emotions, when someone performs an act of goodness to you. Was it an accident that goodness was frequently characterized as a jewel, as a spark, as the light that illumines the human heart?

A little later, the head nurse of the intensive care unit entered the guest room and walked directly toward Dr. Lawson. "Dr. Adams will leave this unit," she said. "There is no need for you to remain in this gloomy place. Janice will accompany him to his room." Dr. Lawson thanked her before leaving the guest room.

"Will I see you tomorrow?" David asked Eve on their way to Dr. Adams's room. "I shall be spending the night with Dr. Adams."

"Yes, I shall see you, and I shall be with you," she said as she moved closer to his right side and held his hand.

No one noticed this conversation mainly because the two lovers were walking behind the group. David pressed Eve's hand. He felt its warmth, and he relished it. For some strange reason, two tears formed in the corners of his eyes. No one should underestimate the power of love. It frees the body and the soul from the social norms imposed on us by society and from all kinds of inhibitions; it allows every fiber of our being to become a means of self-expression. Usually, tears gather in our eyes when feel deep sadness or deep joy, and they usually gather there because these emotions resist expression by ordinary language. Eve desired to speak to David, but she refrained from speaking because she noticed the glitter of those tears. She raised her right hand, wiped them, and hid them in her hand.

David was swelling with love.

"I cannot let those tears fall to the floor, David! They are very hot, they are sweet, and they are sacred!"

FIVE

Master Death's Last Visit to Dr. Adams

Soon after Janice helped Dr. Adams with his breakfast and, more importantly, after he drank a cup of robust coffee, Master Death greeted the celebrated philosopher with a cheerful, and I can say triumphant, "Good morning. I would not visit you at this early hour of the day, Dr. Adams, were I not certain that you would be able to converse with me and that our conversation would enliven your heart and mind. Haven't you always come to life in a serious conversation? Haven't you always delighted in such moments? You may think I am an intruder, but let me assure you that I am a good one! I know that I am Master Death, but I do not hate humanity; on the contrary, I am the humbug that stings human beings in their conscience and stirs them to live up to the promise of the potential that defines their essence and reveals their destiny in this short life of theirs. As I hope to convince you, only when human beings acknowledge the reality of death and live from its standpoint will they live a life filled with anxiety, fear, and loneliness. As your reverend sage taught, a life that does not emanate from the values that are responses to the basic needs of human nature is not worth living. But I can add that such a life is not possible if it is not lived from the standpoint of the reality of death—"

"You have begun to speak in riddles!" Dr. Adams said, interrupting his uninvited guest. "You should not lecture me on what is evident even to philosophy students, even to ordinary people, if you do not persuasively explain the reality of death. How can you say that living from the standpoint of this reality is a condition for leading a worthwhile life if you do not first verify the claim that death is real?"

"The lucidity of your logical mind is truly impressive. I applaud you—"

"I do not need your applause!" Dr. Adams said, again interrupting his uninvited guest.

"But one can neither ignore nor comprehend the finesse of your intellect—of your analytical, critical, and imaginative powers."

"Please get to the point!"

"You have said that the life of a being is a continual process of living death—correct?"

"Yes," Dr. Adams said.

"How can you say that it is a continual process of living death if the human being is still living? In what sense is the living also a dying? What is the referent of 'death' in this context?" Master Death asked.

"It is the continual cessation of the emerging states of being of the human individual. If we mean by 'death' passing out of existence or cessation of being, then 'death' refers to the continual cessation of the being of these states whose totality makes up the life of the human individual. The continual passing away of these states as a whole, when the last state ceases to exist, signifies the death of the human individual. But," Dr. Adams continued, "as a reality in and by itself, death does not exist. I do not encounter it anywhere in the realm of nature or in the realm of my mind, and I do not encounter it anywhere in the past or the future because neither exists. It is simply the cessation of the existence of the last state of being of the individual."

"What you say implies that when a human being exists, it is alive; accordingly, as long as she is alive, the human being is not conscious of her death or nonexistence, nor can she know what it is like to be dead or nonexistent because she cannot perceive the moment of the end of her being. Her death befalls her unawares, so to say. She may suffer, she may tremble when she is conscious of the fact that she will cease to exist, and she may know that death may come at any moment, but she cannot know what it means to die or to cease to exist because she cannot observe that fraction of an instant in which life leaves her—am I correct in drawing this conclusion from what you have just said?"

"Yes," Dr. Adams said.

"But," Master Death responded, "if the life of a human being is a continual process of living death, it should follow that as long as she living, her life would be a process of continually dying and continually emerging from death; otherwise, it could not be a process of living death. But then can the particular human being understand what it means for her life to be a continual process of living death if she does not experience that fraction of an instant before life leaves her?"

"She can understand what it means for her to die because her life is a process of continual dying and continual emerging from this very continual dying. By the power of memory, by which we can recall what happened a moment, a minute, an hour, a day, a week, a month, a year, or many years ago to the present moment of reflection, a moment that lingers into an expanded—stretch of time—now, i.e., present, before the eye of consciousness. During this expanded moment, it is possible to observe the 'now' in an act of immediate intuition or comprehension; it is also possible to discern the transition from the preceding moment that passed away to the succeeding moment that followed it—that is, we discern how the content of a part of the preceding state of being makes a transition into the succeeding state of being and how the other part recedes into the near or distant past, which has ceased to exist in the now, at least to the consciousness of the living individual. The past we normally remember is part, or becomes by the act of memory, a part of the existing present moment.

"But what recedes into the past is part of ourselves. We may recollect it as an idea, as an image, or as an event, and we may not. So far as it is a part, regardless of whether we can recall it into the present as an idea, image, or event, it is practically extinct; therefore, it would be appropriate to say that that element of ourselves is dead. But although it is dead, it is not in a special sense completely dead because it was, directly or indirectly, a formative, dynamical part of ourselves. As Leibnitz noted some centuries ago, no perception we have of the world leaves the domain of our mind. We can, following Freud, say that it is stored in the unconscious domain of the mind. What matters for the present conversation is that in a moment of introspection, the human mind can dwell in the now for an extended period, which we usually experience when we are absorbed in the different social, psychological, aesthetic, religious, intellectual, and personal situations of our daily lives, and we can discern the activity of the passing away of the receding states of our being. Can we really remember anything if we do not assume that we know what it means to remember, that is, what it means for something to recede into the past or into the domain of the being that does not exist in the present? Don't we know what it means for something to be or to have happened in the past, or to make a distinction between the past and the present? But how can we make this distinction if this knowledge is not based on a real understanding of the past in contradistinction to the present and the future?

"The point that merits special attention is that the preceding moment and the succeeding moment intersect in the 'now'; indeed, this very intersection is the locus of the continuity between the past and the present; it is also the occasion that gives rise to the expanded or extended now. For example, when we undergo an aesthetic experience of an artwork, e.g., a literary novel, the novel unfolds before our imagination as a world. We may characterize this world in diverse ways, but what matters is that in this experience, we make a transition from the ordinary world to the aesthetic world of the novel. The aesthetic world is real, and it is more real than the reality of the rocks and animals we encounter in the course of our daily lives. Now, how can we speak of this kind of world if it is not an expanded or extended now? That is, if the preceding moments and the succeeding moments do not fuse into a now in which the distinction between past, present, and future disappears? Isn't this kind of experience an island in the sea of the ordinary world?

"Now," Dr. Adams pressed on, "if you may wonder how this fusion is possible, I can say to you that it is not merely possible; it is real. A physicist can, on the basis of the vector quality of matter, explain how this happens. But this kind of explanation falls outside the parameters of this conversation."

"What do you mean?" Master Death inquired with puzzled eyes.

"I mean this is the nature of time. The idea of past, present, and future is a human construction derived from the way human beings experience time. People constructed its determinations, viz., past, present, and future, because they are units of time and because they experience them in time. They constructed these determinations as a means of organizing their lives. But time in itself is not composed of temporal units or determinations regardless of whether their duration is long or short; it is pure flow or pure process. The universe as a whole or in the abundance of its details is an inexhaustible emanation of this flow. We may characterize this flow in terms of emergence, fulguration, differentiation, creation, radiation, or derivation, as different philosophers have done in the past twenty-five centuries—what matters is that they arise from the endless flow that gives rise to the universe in its amazing diversity.

"The claim that process is the essence of reality does not logically entail any view of its source, purpose, dynamics, or even logic. There is no need for us to explore these questions now. It is only important to recognize that so far as we know and can know, given the power of human cognition, at the particular and cosmic levels, process is the essence of natural and human reality. Philosophers and ordinary people raise the question of the origin or purpose of the cosmic process for personal, religious, explanatory, or personal reasons. For example, they want to know whether the cosmic process is teleological or dysteleological, whether it is administered by a benevolent or indifferent power, or whether this power has any kind relationship to human beings. Nevertheless, regardless of whether such a power exists, it is critically important to recognize that process is the essence of reality. I have focused on this point only because process is the basis of any attempt to understand any aspect of the world of human life.

"Now, if we can experience the passage of time, that is, the transition, which is essentially process, of the preceding and succeeding states of our being—put differently, if we can discern the recession of the preceding states into the world of nonbeing, consequently, if we can know what it means for such a state to recede into the world of nonbeing—it should follow that we can know what it means for the last state of our being to recede into the world of nonbeing. Now let me shed more light on this conclusion, which you tend to contest—"

"I am all ears!" Master Death said with an audible shade of sarcasm. Dr. Adams took in one big gulp of his coffee.

"There is a major difference between the continual recession of the states of our being when we are alive and the recession of the last state, which signifies what I earlier called 'death.' Human beings do not fret or worry much about their mortality when part of their present being recedes into the past or into the world of nonbeing; in fact, they do not pay attention to it. They tend to take it for granted that some of what happens to them or by them today will be buried in the bosom of the past. This is much of the time a healthy attitude. Can you imagine what kind of life you will have if you constantly and simultaneously remember every psychological, social, intellectual, aesthetic, religious, or personal experience you have every day—every second, every minute, every hour, day in and day out? People tend to ignore most of what happens to them or by them daily because this is the general nature of human and natural existence. That which is important in our lives lingers!

"We can say that the basis of this general attitude is habit or faith—the new states that will continue to emerge because we are used to their emergence or because we have faith that they will continue to emerge. But when we get old or terminally ill, or when a devastating accident disrupts the vital functioning of our body permanently, a new consciousness surges from the depth of our mind. We realize that the last state of our being is advancing quickly or that it lurks around the corner. You would argue that the arrival of this last state is not exactly death and that death is something else. But how can it be something else if its recession into nonbeing is the absolute end? What is the ontic difference between extinction and the extinction of the last state of our being?

"Your mind would now wonder, what does it mean to die? Does, or can, the dying person know what it means for her to die? Yes, of course! She knows, or should know, because she has, or should have, acquired this knowledge when she had, or should have, reflected on the process of the continual process of her life, which is a process of continual coming into being and continual reclamation of her being. She did not worry about her continual dying when she was alive because she knew that she would continue to live, of course by dint of habit or faith, but now she worries only because she does not accept the prospect of her absolute end. The source of this worry, which we may characterize as an *absolute concern*, is her conviction that life in general and her life in particular is good. She loved life, and she loved her life more than anything else in the world. Is it an accident that both philosophers and scientists have argued that the strongest impulse in human nature is the impulse to life?

"Thus, if your question is in any way significant, *it should mean or at least it should be cast as, what does it mean to live?*"

"You are a magician!" Master Death exclaimed, interrupting Dr. Adams.

"A magician?" Dr. Adams responded with an expression of bafflement on his face. He took another big sip of coffee and added, "I have tried to show you that death does not exist by the power of argument—no more. If you see any magic in what I said, you should look for it in the power of my argument, not in me."

"Do you mean that logical argument, even if it is the strongest possible kind of argument, can prove the existence or nonexistence of what actually exists? Do you think that you can wipe out my existence by the power of your argument or that you can bring into being a reality from the bosom of nonbeing by the magical wand of your argument?"

"You can believe or disbelieve what you wish, but you cannot convince me that a reality such as death exists if your claim is not supported by compelling logical or empirical argument. If such a reality exists, I should be able to experience it either sensuously or mentally, but I am unable to have this kind of experience. By the way, if you are willing or able to establish the existence of a reality that signifies death when the last state of one's being expires, are you willing to establish a similar reality that signifies the emergence of the first state of one's being or one that signifies the birth and death of every intervening state of being? Even the ancients did not create a god of death. They created a god that oversaw the kingdom of the dead. One more question: I am now standing at the Edge, as you said; can I, do I, experience something called death? And yes, also, as you said, one of my feet is hanging in the land of nonbeing, and even though I am about to be swallowed whole by the cosmic process, the only thing I can feel and can experience is life. If a dying man such as I cannot experience death as a distinct reality, who can? I experience what it means for me to cease to exist, which is tantamount to the extinction of the last state of my being, but I cannot experience something called death."

"You speak as if you are a physical object such as a rock or a mere being, but you are not. You are an unusual complex of ideas, feelings, sensations, instincts, dispositions, powers, hopes, desires, and emotions, and you are a subject that presides over this complex; in short, you are a world of being, of life. During the process of living your life, you enjoyed it and wished from your inmost being that it would endure forever—correct?"

"Yes."

"But your wish will never be fulfilled. Now, when people see for the first time the shadow of death slowly emerging from around the corner, they are gripped by fear and trepidation. This shadow means that the last state of their being is about to expire—correct?"

"Yes."

"This realization is prompted by a peculiar predicament—"

"A predicament!" Adams ejaculated.

"Yes, the predicament of all predicaments!" Dr. Adams's eyes widened with an obvious expression of expectation. "It is the moment people," Master Death continued, "and now you, stand between two solid, impenetrable walls, the wall of being and the wall of nonbeing, which you almost see with the eyes of your mind. What can one do in this very narrow, oppressive space? The only thing one can do is open up the door of her past, which exists for her as an idea, as a representation, and to use a contemporary analogue, as a movie. She feels that she has no choice but to watch this movie. Different people react to it differently. There is no need to survey their reactions, but I would not be too much amiss if I say that all of them would lament and many would regret, sorely regret, their imminent departure from this world, regardless of whether the life they lived was poor, mediocre, great, or magnificent. It is their personal world, after all! Who does not value this world and try keep it alive forever?

"In this moment of reflection, the dying person cannot but recognize that her imminent death is really the absence of a *human world* from the world of being of something good, good in itself, as you argued in a few of your lectures on the meaning of human life. For her, her death is not merely the cessation of the existence of the last state of her life but the absence of something good from the world. The good should not perish, and yet her life, which is a supreme good, is perishing before her eyes. She cannot experience the extinction of the last state of her being, but she can experience the absence, which is a mode of nonbeing, of her own life. As far as she is concerned, this absence is the highest form of evil. Let me here emphasize to you, Dr. Adams, that in this episode of reflection on her life, which practically ceased to exist since it is buried in the belly of the past, she recognizes the meaning of her impending extinction, she explores it, and she understands what it means for her to die. She can do this because she can feel and discern the absence of the totality of her life. This feeling and discernment enable her to see what it is like to be extinct. This is not an abstract but a living feeling and discernment. It is an experience of death. It is not an experience of the cessation of the last state of her life but the gradual unfolding of her own death, the death that began to take place from the moment she was born to this present moment. Again, the experience of this unfolding of her living death is the distinctive mark of the experience of death. People do not experience it after they die but during their lifetime, when they are living and dramatically when they approach the end. Oh, Dr. Adams, how many a human being dies before she is born—of course, as a human being, not as a lump of flesh? How many a man or a woman suffers the agony of their own of their death in moments of devastation? Don't they see with their own eyes the actuality of their recession into the land of human living? Don't they experience nonbeing in the heart of their being? Don't moments of tragedy, of catastrophe, of total destruction reveal the reality of death in a moment of epiphany? How could Saint Shakespeare's

Hamlet say in a dramatic, earthshaking moment that the question is to be or not to be if he did not see the very death of his own being? How can any human being make such a confession, not on an artistic stage but on the stage of human life, if she has not witnessed the real face of death?

"Let me cite a conversation between a distinguished architect dying from terminal cancer and one of his dear friends. 'If I knew I were dying, especially if I knew what it means to die the way I now know it, the way I now feel death crawling through my veins, the way it is eating me up slowly, I would have lived my life quite differently. The life I have led was the wrong life. Notice how I used the past tense "had" only because I have no life anymore; right now, I am simply existing! I am talking about my life as a person. I had been postponing my real life one stretch at a time as if I were going to live forever. But my only solace, which is not a solace, is that I did not know any better.' Hasn't this human being seen and so experienced his absence, and you can say his own extinction, from this world? How could he have made this kind of confession had he not experienced the meaning of his absence from the world of reality?

"Let me here assure you that absence, especially the absence of a human being, can be experienced. A lover says to his beloved who has been away for a while, 'I missed you so much, my dear!' Let us suppose that this man is honest in what he said; what did he mean by 'missed you'? Or in what sense did he miss his beloved? Could he have missed her if she were not present him, if she were not a living reality in his experience while she was away? Again, could he have missed her if he had not experienced her absence? His experience of her absence is not an experience of nothing but of her absence from his life. It is a concrete experience. If his experience of her absence had been vacuous, he could not have missed her because nothing is complete silence and so cannot be experienced. His experience of her absence is an experience of her presence in her absence. If she were not such a presence, his confession would have been a strike of flattery, if not a strike of hypocrisy. The difference between the experience of this kind of absence and the experience of the absence of one's life from the world of being is that the first is temporary and the second is permanent.

"Now if, as you said, a human being is a continual process of living death, she must also be a continual process of reclamation of life, or being. The existential consciousness of this incontrovertible fact should be the basis of human life; that is, it should be the basis of planning and living one's life. You may wonder, how? My answer is simple:

"The existential consciousness of the fact that the human being is a continual process of dying and reclamation of her life and that this process will end after a certain period, long or short, *should incline the human being* to live from the standpoint of this dual fact. I underline this claim only because the majority, if not all, of the people now and in the past conduct or conducted their lives on the erroneous assumption that they would live forever, the way the architect did. This is a main reason most of them practically lead mediocre, unfulfilled lives. Oh, they live and they believe that theirs is the best possible life, but they are not aware that they live more as sheep in a herd, as contended sheep, than as the shepherds of their lives, as human individuals, as individuals who live from the core of their humanity. Why would a man like the architect, who is one of the majority of the people who do not live from the core of their humanity, regret the life he had chosen when he suddenly found himself standing on the Edge? If I know that my life is short, why would I waste it? Would I waste any minute of it? Wouldn't I squeeze the juice of joy that comes from a productive, meaningful, truly human way of life? A life of hard but productive work is a source of the greatest pleasure people can relish as human beings. The pleasure of the indolent, the mediocre, is a shallow kind of pleasure. It is momentary and leaves behind a vacant, lonely soul!" Master Death said and threw a jubilant look at Dr. Adams as if he were the man who had conquered Planet Earth! This look spoke loudly, and its thrust reached Dr. Adams's ears with a bang.

An inner voice, one that rises from the depth of the logical mind, returned a sober, thoughtful look at his uninvited guest, or perhaps imposter. The line of reasoning Dr. Adams had just heard, which was impressive, came from a person who knew the course of human civilization and the history of ideas. Although he was not quite aware of it, Dr. Adams had been challenged by this guest. His body was deteriorating, and he was losing his strength rather rapidly. But he never shrank from a debate, and he never gave up until the very end.

"Don't worry, Dr. Adams," Master Death said. "I know you are weak, and I know that your second foot is moving closer to the Edge, and I know that your strength is waning faster than you thought. I shall not interfere in the course of nature. I suggest that you take a painkiller. Your beloved Janice left a few tablets in this cabinet." Master Death opened the cabinet and brought a painkiller to the dying man. "Have it!" He cast a serene glance at Dr. Adams and added, "I am truly anxious to see how you are going to show me that I do not exist even though we are having a serious conversation! I said that you are an amazing human being. I am just anxious to see how your brilliance will reveal itself before you say good farewell to you friends!"

Contrary to Master Death's recommendation, Dr. Adams declined the pill. Pain had never deterred him from achieving his projects; it was always under his control, and it was under his control at that critical moment of his life. It may seem difficult for some people to know that, whether in science, philosophy, art, religion, social reform, or even ordinary life, the genuine creator is indifferent to pain and that she is indifferent to public opinion regardless of whether it is good or bad, true or false. Instead of taking the medication, he took a big gulp of his robust coffee. It was cold! He did not feel its coldness. All the power of his mind was focused on the intruder's line of reasoning. Instead of looking at him, Dr. Adams looked into the infinite space that separated them and said:

"Your response can be divided into two parts. In the first, you advanced a twofold argument in support of your claim that death is real. In the second, you explained the advantage of creating an existential consciousness of death in the mind of the human being. Though briefly, we have considered the second part. Your argument for the reality of death is our concern in this conversation. Let me at once state that your line of reasoning is invalid—"

Master Death frowned, and a feeling of deep dissatisfaction loomed over his face. He really thought that the argument he had developed for Dr. Adams was decisive, final, and that their conversation was practically concluded. But he was mistaken because Dr. Adams, a reputed debater, advanced the following reasons for his rejection of Master Death's line of reasoning:

"First, your claim that if the human being is a continual process of living death, which I articulated in a particular conceptual context earlier, and next, if the human being can experience the continual recession of the states of being in this process because she can contemplate the continual emergence and passing away of these states, it would be possible for her to discern and experience the death as well as the emergence of her states of being. This is why you were able to say that a person can know what it means to experience death during her lifetime.

"The primary proposition of this argument, which you expanded in some detail, is that one can recognize the receding states of one's being because some parts of them are transmitted into the succeeding states of being of the living human being. She recognizes the past states and their recession by remembering their identity, and she can recognize their identity because they lingered in the succeeding states. But if they do not linger in the succeeding states of the being of the person, it would be impossible for her to recognize them; consequently, she would not be able to know that they have passed into nonbeing or that they are transmitted into the emerging states of her being. She can recognize them only because she can remember them; she cannot discern some of them in the succeeding states, and if she does, she can do this *in terms of the present states of being, those that have lingered in the succeeding states*. Delete these states and you undercut the possibility of recognizing them as coming into being. Without this memory, the activity of recognition does not happen. What you seem to overlook is that she experiences the preceding states as past states in terms of her memory of them, which she discerned in the states that have been transmitted into the succeeding states. Again, without this memory, she would not be able to remember or recognize the past states.

"But you see, one cannot experience the passing out of the final state of one's being because she will cease to exist the instant that state expires; consequently, she cannot know what it means for her to die or to experience what it means for her to cease to exist. She certainly understands what it means to live because she can experience, as we have just seen, the process of her continual living and dying, but she cannot understand what it means for her to die because she cannot experience the moment of her extinction. As I said at the beginning of the conversation, that moment signifies the cessation of her being. Once she dies, she cannot return to discern what it was like for the moment to take place.

"You commit the same mistake in the second part of your twofold argument, namely, the argument from the experience of absence, or the experience of presence in absence. You have said that, broadly speaking, 'absence' signifies the nonbeing of an object; but although it signifies nonbeing, it can be experienced. This essentially means that one can experience absence or nonbeing because she can experience the presence of the object in its absence. *Prima facie*, this strikes one as a contradictory proposition. This is based on the assumption that the logic of reality does not always conform to the laws of formal logic. But I think you are aware of the contradictory aspect of your proposition, and so you tried to justify its validity on experiential grounds. I shall assume the reasonableness of your assumption for the sake of argument.

"Suppose my beloved goes with a team of archaeologists to examine the remains of an ancient culture in one of our mountains; suppose she spends two months around the site of the remains; finally, suppose the first urgent emotion I express when she returns from her trip is, 'I missed you so much, my dear!' When I make this statement, I certainly mean that she was present to me during her absence. I experience her presence in her absence, i.e., I experience her nonexistence during her absence; otherwise, it would be idle to say that I missed her: How can I undergo the experience of missing her if she is absent from my consciousness now? The idea you tried to elaborate or defend is that I am able to say 'I miss you' because I can envision the totality of our life together until the moment she left me. This slice of our life lingers not merely in my memory as a mental state but also as an integral part of my being because to have an experience of 'missing' her is essentially an existential experience. Here actual presence ceased to exist the moment she left me. Her departure left a vacuum in my being, but despite this vacuum, she is present. Now, in what sense is she present? As an idea? As an enlivened past presence? As a memory? According to you, I should know what it means for her to be absent because I can conjure up or envision the totality of the past presence in my mind and imagine its non-existence the moment she left me. But how can I imagine her nonexistence when she does not actually exist? Making such a statement implies that I imagine her nonexistence in terms of the absence of her past presence, which is no more than a mental state. I know what it means for her to be absent because I know what it means for her to be present. Fine! But do I in this sense experience her absence or nonexistence? No, because her nonex-istence is not an object of my reflection or observation. The only thing I can experience is her past presence, which I do not now have and which I desire to have. In other words, I experience my desire for her past presence, which was dear to me. Thus, when I say that I know what it means for my beloved to be absent, what I can or should mean is that I long for what I did have. The basis of this longing, which is an assertion, is her past presence, which lingers in me as a part of my inner self. Memory is the basis of this experi-ence. I experience her absence in terms of the memory of her past presence.

"But what if her absence is permanent—does the length of her ab-sence change the structure of the argument? No. I can keep longing for her because the content of her past presence lingers in my being. Don't husbands and wives, friends, even family members gradually lose the feeling of longing when they become certain that the absence of the loved ones will be permanent? But regardless of whether the absence is permanent, we know what it means for an object, human or natural, to be absent in terms of their past presence. This means that their absence is the absence of their past presence. Their present absence or nonexistence is not an object of experience or nonbeing.

"Let me now remind you of what I stated at the beginning of our conversation: 'death' signifies the end of the life or existence of a husband living or existing reality. It is not a reality that exists in and by itself. We can talk about only life or existence and what it means for this life or existence to cease to exist—"

"But how can you talk about it apart from a serious consideration of this end?" Master Death snapped.

"The experience of the end is, as I have already argued, an ongoing experience because life is an ongoing experience of this end and its reclamation, as the later metaphysicians of the last century argued. We know, or can know, what it means to die because we know what it means for it to end, and we know what it means for it to end because this knowledge is based on an ongoing experience in every existing moment of our living process in this short life of ours. Now, if death does not exist, you cannot be its embodiment, for an end cannot be an embodiment; it signifies the end of a reality, but it is not a reality. It is more appropriate to say that it is an aspect of reality.

"If you are not an embodiment of death, since death does not exist, you cannot be Master Death, and if you cannot be Master Death, who are you? Speak!"

Master Death frowned, curled his lips inward as if he were tackling a difficult mathematical problem, and then said with an obviously haughty attitude, "I am one of the devil's offspring. You know my father well, and you should know that he is the father of separation, of destruction, of the extinction of everything that exists."

Dr. Adams listened to these words with a thoughtful and tranquil state of mind and refocused his attention on the face of the intruder the way he focused his attention on the face of his father some years ago. Like his father, this anomaly was an intruder. His father was an enemy of love and this offspring was an enemy of life. Dr. Adams pursed his lips lightly and decided to listen to what the intruder had to say. Anyway, he was weak, he was tired, and he had lost his enthusiasm to prolong his conversation with such a being.

"You denied the reality of death," Master Death continued. "You argued that death signifies the end of a reality. Your arguments were compelling, the way your arguments and commitment to truth with my father were compelling. My father warned me that you are a formidable debater. He was right. I do not wish to flatter you if I repeat what I said at the beginning of our visit—"

"Visit? No! Encounter? Yes!"

"'Encounter' is fine. Given my nature, I do not see any difference between a visit and an encounter," Master Death said. "I am serious when I say that you deserve the utmost respect and admiration even though neither I nor my father likes you! You command this respect and admiration against my better judgment. But it is prudent to continue this conversation for a few more minutes only because that detestable Janice, that flare of mushy love, will be bringing several medicines and another container of oxygen shortly. I cannot stand that woman. Like you, she is my enemy. Her primary aim as a nurse and as a person is promotion of love—building what my father and I are trying to destroy. You see, you are a monument of love. My aim was to destroy this monument—"

"Stop this nonsense!" Dr. Adams said, interrupting Master Death. Frankly, he had lost his patience with this insolent intruder!

"Dr. Adams, you reduced death to a word that signifies the end of the being of a reality. But you have not asked yourself, what brings about this end? Why do all realities that make up the structure of the cosmic process come to a final end? Neither you nor any mind can explain the existence of such a cause. If your Heraclitus wisely stated that things come to an end, I can ask, what makes them come to an end? You may advance explanations of the intermediary events that come to an end, but you cannot dismiss the need to explain or posit a primary cause. Even your philosophical forefathers acknowledged this need. But what they and their successors failed to do is to show that my father as the supreme destructive force is immanent in the essence of every element of the cosmic process. I am an embodiment of this force. I am responsible for the birth and death of every human being who exists."

"You may or you may not be such a force, for it is obvious that death is a fact of all existence; but let me assure you that now I do not, and shall not, experience anything called death. All I shall experience until the moment of my extinction is life and nothing else. It does not matter whether the remainder of my life, which is very imminent, is poor, happy, painful, or glorious; what matters is that it is life, period. Nothing else exists for me. You can kill me now, but if you do, the act of killing me will end my life sooner rather than later."

"When my father left you last time, he sprayed you with three curses. I spray you with the same three curses," Master Death said. He then spat on Dr. Adams and vanished.

Dr. Adams closed his eyes and leaned against the half-raised bed. He was in a daze, perhaps a deep reverie. He felt as if he were lost in a dense, dark forest, moving among its trees and bushes without knowing where he was going or how to find his way into the world of light. He was anxious to know the meaning of that anomalous encounter. Although the intruder had identified himself as Master Death, although he had argued shrewdly in support of the reality of death, although he had exhibited supernatural powers that hardly any rational being would believe, and although he had confessed at the end of his intrusive visit that he was an offspring of the devil, of the destructive force in the universe, Dr. Adams was truly baffled by this strange amalgam of a being. But he sank into that daze for another reason. He was truly baffled by the show of supernatural powers he had witnessed, the rational restraint of the intruder, and the fierceness of the duel he had had with him. Had the visits of Master Death been episodes of hallucination? Had they been real? Who would believe Dr. Adams if he were to reveal them to his friends? But goodness, who would refuse to believe him either? The conversations he had conducted with the intruder and the vast knowledge of the history of ideas and human nature the intruder had revealed betrayed a human mind no one could either doubt or underestimate.

But, regardless of whether those visits had been hallucinations, Dr. Adams felt an inner, irresistible inclination to reflect on the substance and especially on the meaning of these visits. Indeed, despite their fictional, intrusive, and supernatural character, they were in a strict sense meaningful because they were rationally conducted and because they focused on one of the most important questions of the meaning of human life: how should human beings live and die as human beings? We cannot examine the question of the meaning of human life without a serious examination of the question of the reality and meaning of death, as the conversations clearly revealed. But alas, is there or can there be a more important question people should answer? We may create the greatest works of art, we may advance the most useful theories of science, we may create the most sophisticated human and industrial technologies, we may construct the most enlightening philosophical and theological systems, we may design the best system of government, we may devise the most interesting means of entertainment, yes, and we may create the most rational system of education—why? I raise this question because it arises from the bosom of human experience in all the preceding modes of human endeavor or striving. Suppose we reflect on this question the way Dr. Adams did; what might the context of the answer to this question be but human life? What does it mean to be a human being? Under what conditions can one live as a human being? Again, what might the thrust of this context be but an adequate articulation of these conditions? As Dr. Adams emphasized to Dr. Lawson, the question is, how can one lead a fulfilled human life? The urgency of this question intensifies, and in fact acquires a dramatic character, when we existentially recognize, as Dr. Adams did, that human life is short. This dramatic character intensifies still more when we also recognize that the human dimension of our being is not given to us as a ready-made reality but as a reality to be realized by us as particular individuals. Under what conditions can we become the human individuals we should be in this short life?

I am not unaware of the fact that many people answer this question differently. This difference stems from their different social, cultural, religious, ideological, economic, and educational backgrounds. Many people do not realize the kind of satisfaction they are capable of as human beings. They enjoy a few crumbs of pleasures and view them as all the satisfaction they are capable of, which is a blunder. As Dr. Adams lucidly explained, the satisfaction we should seek in our lives consists of meeting the essential needs human nature demands—the physical, aesthetic, religious, intellectual, cultural, emotional, and professional needs. Meeting these needs adequately is the basis of leading a well-rounded human life.

It is sad that most people raise the question of all questions of human life at the end, when they approach the Edge, not at the beginning—when it is late, when their time on this earth is up! Why? This sad state of the human condition stood prominently, almost provocatively, at the forefront of Dr. Adams's consciousness when he sank into that deep daze the instant the intruder vanished from his presence. Why would a human being with one leg hanging in the world of nonbeing worry, or should we say care, about this aspect of the human condition? Perhaps we should care about the well-being of human beings in general, that is, about beings we do not even know? Why do the physicist, the artist, the social reformer, the teacher, the priest, the philosopher, and the inventor consume their lives in a concerted effort to discover the truth of human nature and seek it? Why does the social reformer devote her life to promote social justice, freedom, and peace in the lives of people? Why are some of them willing to die rather than give up their quest?

But where can an adequate answer to this question be found, much less gleaned? I think that the locus of our search should be the essential structure of human nature, as Dr. Adams recommended. I emphasize this point because the question of all questions is not the privilege or task of the philosopher or the scientist, the parent, the teacher, or the legislator but of every human being. The question is how this unique human individual should live, not how an abstract individual who exists in the mind of the philosopher or psychologist as an idea should live. This is exactly why Dr. Adams proposed that the primary aim of liberal education should be the cultivation of human character—one that can think, feel, will, and act on its own without external support; one that knows the meaning and significance of beauty, goodness, truth, and the joy of living. But the question that was pestering Dr. Adams at that critical moment of his life, perhaps more than any other question, was, why should the cultivated human being who lives from the core of her humanity *care* about other human beings? Is the obligation to care about other people a natural impulse? If it is, what credit does she receive or what satisfaction should she feel when she cares for someone? Is this kind of obligation a moral obligation? If it is, how can it be justified? Is it a matter of choice? Even if it is an obligation, is it prudent for one to care for others in a ruthless, selfish, uncaring world, one that does not even recognize the worth or value of the moral act or life?

Dr. Adams was still trying to find his way through this thorny thicket of questions when Janice stood next to his bed and gaped into his closed eyes. Although they were closed, they were not peaceful, nor did they indicate a peaceful state of mind, not only because their lids were tense but also because his lips were closed tightly. At first, she thought that the cause of his discomfort was lack of oxygen, for she noted that the tubes that were inserted in his nostrils had fallen a little, but she was mistaken because, having felt her presence, he opened his eyes, and as he always did, he smiled. But this time his smile was not as pure, as lively, and as warm as it had always been. She felt that something physical or psychological had been troubling him. She held his hand and pressed it gently to her cheek. The warmth of that touch, of that human touch, the touch that was blessed by the fire of the human heart, glided into his heart and mind. Two tears glittered in the corners of his eyes. He could not speak, but those tears spoke. Janice saw their glitter and felt the warmth of his heart. For a strange reason, he felt that his end was near. This feeling was enforced by the realization that Dr. Hardy was supposed to come but did not. He had always kept his promises. Dr. Adams reflected on the doctor's absence for a few seconds. He could not help but feel that his former student did not come only because he could not bear the sight of his teacher's departure from the world. Involuntarily, he asked, "Dr. Hardy?" Janice understood the purport of this question, but she could not answer him. He was right. Dr. Adams did not press her. A kaleidoscope of emotions, images, ideas, and human scenes swarmed his consciousness. He was unable to reflect on all of them, but one question, the same question that had pestered him a moment ago, was dominant: What makes this woman, this warm heart, a flame of care? Why does she give it freely, abundantly, unconditionally? Do I deserve this divine gift? Is she really morally obligated to care for me—this way? It cannot be! Master Death had performed before his eyes a few supernatural acts, which would befuddle the minds of some, if not all, human beings. But such acts, he thought, paled in significance in the presence of the grandeur of this flame of care! This kind of flame was miraculous, more miraculous than anything we would do in our lifetime.

Dr. Adams looked again at Janice and dwelled on her presence. Those tears gave birth to a flood of tears. Janice pulled a tissue from a small box sitting on the side table and wiped them tenderly. If only Janice knew, or could know, the depth of Dr. Adams's mind and heart! If only she knew the wealth of loving emotions that were striving to leave that heart and mind, and stream into hers! Yes, had she known the magnitude of that wealth, her mind would have witnessed the supernatural powers of her flame of care and the surge of the love that was striving to flow into his heart. Alas! Can this kind of flame and this kind of surge originate from a feeling of moral obligation? Acts of love are not acts of moral obligation. They are divine acts.

But why should the heart that swells with this kind of love stand on the Edge? Why should it perish? Can the divine perish? Dr. Adams did not and could not contemplate, much less raise, this and the other questions that were buzzing in his mind. How could he? Does the spring ask itself, why do I give water to the plants or the arid land? Does the sun ask itself, Why do I give light to the world? Does the mother who is willing to die for her sick child ask herself, Why am I willing to die for my child? The existence of the divine is absolute. The absolute resists even considering such questions! By its very essence, it is pure flow, pure giving.

❋ ❋ ❋ ❋ ❋

The human being is a world! She is an unusually rich mosaic of beliefs, values, hopes, aspirations, desires, dreams, experiences, powers, emotions, feelings—yes, a world that cannot be communicated in the fullness of its being, not even to one's self. Two human worlds were throbbing with life when David and Eve moved into Dr. Adams's room with inquisitive eyes and anxious hearts. Both of them had decided to skip their classes that day and if need be the whole week. They felt an urgent desire to be with the man who stood as a brilliant tower in their lives. No one knew that they had decided to skip their classes that day, as if their minds and hearts had already begun to think and feel synergistically. The logic of innocence, of the pure heart and mind, is one and the same everywhere in the world. These two lovers were not an exception. They met in the parking lot of the hospital. Their parents and Janice did not know how they had met that morning, and they did not know or entertain the idea that they had exchanged romantic expressions, that they had held each other's hands, or that they had embraced when they faced each other in that lonely parking lot of the hospital. No one knew how they had met, and no knew whether they had embraced, shaken hands, greeted each other verbally, or allowed their lips to feel their mutual longing for each other. We may wonder about this kind of magnificent, magical, and precious encounter between lovers because, from their point of view, the flame of love that burns in their hearts is sacred. No one can tread or trespass on this kind of sacred land.

Yes, the world that thrived in Dr. Adams's heart and mind was throbbing with life when those two flames of love approached his bed. Before they reached it, Janice, the good Janice, rose to her feet and hugged them. She knew that they were spiritual emanations of the man she loved and respected. She saw him in them. Love is a mirror that reflects the heart of the person who loves. Oh, how grand is this kind of love! She investigated their faces as she was freeing them from her hug. Her eyes emanated a flood of sadness; she looked at them and she smiled, also a smile of sadness. The lovers saw, felt, and understood that Dr. Adams's final moment was near, very near. They stood together next to his bed.

"Good morning, Uncle Seneca!" Eve said and then bent over his body and kissed him on the cheek, as she always did, but this time her kiss lingered for a long time. She could not resist the flow of some tears over his cheeks.

"Good morning to you, my dear," he said when her lips left his cheek.

Janice, who was watching this scene with tears in her eyes, pulled out a tissue from a small box sitting on the side table and wiped her tears. Dr. Adams did not see this scene of the two women weeping because David had already moved closer to Dr. Adams's bed with a "Good morning." Like Eve, he could not resist a determined desire to kiss his teacher on his cheek, and he could not resist the flow of tears over his own cheeks either. His lips trembled. He wished to express to him the magnitude of his love, respect, and gratitude for him, but he could not. His trembling lips stifled the possibility of such expression. Dr. Adams saw those tears flowing on his cheeks, and he saw those lips trembling.

"Come closer, David!" he said. David did. "Closer! Your head!" David lowered his head. Dr. Adams kissed him on both cheeks. "Do not forget my recommendation," Dr. Adams said in a whisper

"No sir! It is already done!"

Dr. Adams smiled. His eyes emanated a ray of joy. Then he asked Eve to come closer to him the way he had asked David a few seconds ago. "Love!" he whispered in her ear.

Eve, whose heart was aflame with two contradictory feelings, of joy and sadness, whispered back, "Yes, Uncle Seneca. We are!"

Dr. Adams leaned on his half-raised bed and gazed into the ceiling of his room for a few moments. A soft smile, a smile of peace, settled in the corner of his mouth. Priests, philosophy professors, and parents preach the gospel of love. They glorify it, and they do their best to assure the young and the old that love is the royal road to true happiness. But for some strange reason, true love seems to be the sparest reality in human life. And yet the urge for this kind of love is one of the strongest urges in human nature. Is love really an art, as some philosophers and psychologists have argued? But alas, can art be taught? Suppose true love is an art; can one teach it if one is not an artist? We may be able to teach the meaning or conditions under which it can be practiced, but we cannot teach anyone how to love the way we teach mathematics, chemistry, or geology. Again, if art in general could be taught, most friendships, marriages, and the various types of human relationships would not fail. The only way we can enable a person to love is to love that person and to keep loving her until she sees and understands how to love—that is, until she is able to see it for what it is, to make her feel its sweetness, pain, and true worth. How do people fall in love? By exchanging gifts, kisses, even sexual satisfaction, or by being a shining example of love? But how can we do this except by what we do or achieve in our personal, professional, social, and family lives? *Is it an accident that in a situation of love, the heart feels what the eyes see, and the eyes see what the heart feels?*

Dr. Adams was a torch of love. Most of the people who met him, those who witnessed him with the eyes of their hearts and minds, saw the light of this torch. How can you close your eyes when you are in its presence? How can you prevent its light from seeping into your very being? Is it an accident that people fall in love? You can broker a marriage, you can have a semblance of love for a price, or you can be deceived into one, *but falling into it* means living its fire and is something else! To Dr. Adams, romantic love is human love par excellence. The difference between the two is that romantic love is a relation of total giving and receiving between the lovers. They share everything they have or possess, material and spiritual, even their bodies.

No one present in the room knew exactly why Dr. Adams sank into that daze, and no one knew why his face was a radiance of peace. He was tired, and he was physically ready to leave. He knew it, and he willed it. There was no need for him to justify his decision only because there was no need to justify his existence. Why do you need to justify your life before your conscience if you have led a fulfilled life? Dr. Adams's life was a fulfilled life! On the contrary, as far as I know, he was about to leave it with a feeling of gratitude! Again, he was not afraid to leave this world—how can you be afraid to leave it if the life you have lived was good?

During that lull, Janice left her patient and the two lovers and went to her office to see if she was needed for an urgent task and to replenish some of Dr. Adams's medications. Dr. Adams was still napping. The two lovers gazed into his peaceful face for a few long moments and then at each other. David could not lift his eyes off the face of his beloved teacher. Unaware of what he was doing, he moved closer to Eve and embraced her tightly, then more tightly. She felt him—his very soul! "Oh, my love! I wish—" he began to whisper in her ear.

"I wish your wish, David!" she said, interrupting him. "Your wish is burning in my heart. My wish is on fire; I am on fire! Oh, don't leave me!"

"How can I leave you if you are my heart? How can I leave you without my heart, without the fire of my life? How can I breathe without my heart? I shall always live from this fire with you, and I shall die in it! Nothing can sunder me from you!" David kept his arm around her for a long time, a time that seemed to both of them like an eternity; then he held her shoulders with his hands, gaped deeply into her eyes, placed his left cheek on her right cheek, and pressed it softly. A short moment later, she slowly moved her cheek away from his and placed her lips on his. Two flames of fire were united into one. Their lips were sealed in their hearts by this fire. But their kiss did not last long because they heard the sound of wheels moving in the direction of the room. They sat on their chairs and waited for the entry of those wheels.

Janice entered with a small cart covered with several small containers of medications, bags, and bottles of water. "You must be hungry! It is lunchtime," she said in a hardly audible voice to the innocent-looking lovers. And in fact they were innocent! Is love a crime?

With one voice, the lovers said, also in a hardly audible voice, a determined no. When Janice heard this harmonious response, when she felt the melody of the concord between them, she cast a special glance at them. Alas! Their cheeks were covered with a crimson blush! She understood, and although she was roasting in the pain of her sadness, she felt very happy for them. How could she withstand this feeling if they were beloved by the man she loved?

But this diversion was immediately followed by another diversion. Dr. Lawson and Jasmine tiptoed their way into the room. They moved directly to their daughter. Jasmine hugged her. Wow! Eve's body was flaming! She looked into her face. It was ruddy. Her eyes were aglow with a special effulgence. Jasmine's fear that her daughter might be feeling unwell was instantly transformed into a feeling of gladness, of thrill, when her eyes caught sight of David's face.

Dr. Lawson, who did not interrupt his wife's embrace with his daughter, moved to Dr. Adams's bed. But for a mysterious reason, Dr. Adams slowly opened his eyes. Was it the scent of his friend, his spiritual presence, or some kind of telepathic communion? But does it really matter? Isn't human presence a spiritual power that penetrates the most solid walls on earth? "Stanley!" Dr. Adams said and took in a deep breath. "I knew you would come. I could not leave before seeing you one more time, before touching you, before feeling your sweet presence, my friend!"

"Oh no, you are not leaving!" Dr. Lawson almost cried.

"I am. It is time. No one can argue with Father Time! You know this fact more than anyone in this city."

"Oh no!" Dr. Lawson murmured.

"Jasmine!" Dr. Adams said softly. He took her hand and kissed it. With tears in his eyes and a painful sob leaving his throat sluggishly, he turned his face toward Janice. "Let me feel you, my dear!" Janice bent her body over his expiring body and tried to kiss him, but he intercepted her gesture and kissed her on the lips with more tears in his eyes. He took in one more breath and then tried to speak with David and Eve, but his lungs had already collapsed.

Melancholy enfolded Dr. Adams's friends when the candle that had shone in their lives was dimmed by the hand of time. They could neither speak nor move for a few seconds.

"Janice, please, you and David join us for a drink and supper in memory of Dr. Adams, our friend," said Jasmine.

"This is his wish." Dr. Lawson said. "His body will be cremated tomorrow morning at five o'clock."

Except for Janice, who went to her office to complete some legal forms regarding Dr. Adams's death, Dr. Lawson, Jasmine, David, and Eve went back to school.

But the wheel of Time kept turning on, as it has always done, indifferent to the feelings, desires, or projects of human beings or any other type of being.

www.ingramcontent.com/pod-product-compliance
Lightning Source LLC
Chambersburg PA
CBHW070821250626
47170CB00006B/2179